PHILIP ALLAN

LITERATURE GUIDE

FOR GCSE

AQA ANTHOLOGY: MOON ON THE TIDES

CONFLICT AND RELATIONSHIPS

Margaret Newman

With thanks to Karen Chester for reviewing the manuscript of this book

Philip Allan Updates, an imprint of Hodder Education, an Hachette UK company, Market Place, Deddington, Oxfordshire OX15 0SE

Orders

Bookpoint Ltd, 130 Milton Park, Abingdon, Oxfordshire OX14 4SB
tel: 01235 827827
fax: 01235 400401
e-mail: education@bookpoint.co.uk
Lines are open 9.00 a.m.–5.00 p.m., Monday to Saturday, with a 24-hour message answering service. You can also order through the Philip Allan Updates website: www.philipallan.co.uk

© Philip Allan Updates 2010
ISBN 978-1-4441-1028-9
First printed 2010

Impression number 5 4 3 2
Year 2015 2014 2013 2012 2011

Cover photograph reproduced by permission of Trinity Mirror/Mirrorpix/Alamy
Page graphic courtesy of ImageDJ/Cadmium

Printed in Spain

Hachette UK's policy is to use papers that are natural, renewable and recyclable products and made from wood grown in sustainable forests. The logging and manufacturing processes are expected to conform to the environmental regulations of the country of origin.

Contents

Introduction

This guide is intended for you to use throughout your GCSE English literature course. It will help you when you are studying the poems for the first time and also during your revision. It explores in detail all the poems in the 'Conflict' and 'Relationships' clusters in your anthology. There is also advice on how to compare the poems and how to make sure you demonstrate the correct skills when writing about them. Enjoy referring to the guide, and good luck in your exam.

Features of this guide

The following features have been used throughout this guide:

● **Which aspects of the poem should I compare?**	**Introductory questions** are provided at the beginning of some sections. Check you have understood each of these before you move on.

Grade *booster* **!**	Pay particular attention to the **Grade booster** boxes. Students with a firm grasp of these ideas are likely to be aiming for the top grades.

Pause for thought **II**	Develop your thinking skills by answering questions in the **Pause for thought** boxes. You might gain extra insight into the poem.

Key quotation 'Love's time's beggar' ('Hour')	Highlighted for you are **key quotations** that you may wish to use as evidence in your examination answers.

Grade *focus* **!**	To help you give a higher-level response, **Grade focus** boxes compare responses at different levels.

Review your learning	Test your knowledge after you have read some of the sections in the **Review your learning** boxes. Answers are available to download at **www.philipallan.co.uk/literatureguidesonline**.

 Don't forget to go online for further self-tests on the poems: **www.philipallan.co.uk/literatureguidesonline**. You can also find more exam responses at grade C and A* and a glossary of literary terms.

How to approach poetry

A poet's work is to name the unnameable, to point at frauds, to take sides, start arguments, shape the world, and stop it from going to sleep.

Salman Rushdie

Of our conflicts with others we make rhetoric; of our conflicts with ourselves we make poetry.

William Butler Yeats

Poetry was never written to be studied in an examination. It has always been written — and will continue to be written — to explore ideas and emotions and inspire us. The examiners who chose the poems for the anthology themes have tried to offer you a wide selection of experiences, introducing you to famous poets from our literary heritage, as well as an interesting variety of contemporary poets.

When you meet a new poem for the first time, do not try to solve it as though it is a puzzle testing your intelligence. Instead, read it through a few times, perhaps read it aloud, and get a feel for what it is trying to say. It does not matter if there are words you do not understand. Plato, the classical Greek philosopher, is reported to have said: 'Poets utter great and wise things which they do not themselves understand.'

What does matter in the exam is that you are able to give a personal response to the poems you write about, using the poets' skills to present your opinions. The poets were not afraid to express their ideas, so don't be afraid to express yours.

How to use this guide

You may find it useful to read sections of this guide when you need them, rather than reading it from start to finish. For example, you may find it useful to read the notes and information on individual poems in your chosen theme shortly after you have read the poem for the first time. The sections *Comparing poems* and *Tackling the assessments* will be especially useful in the weeks leading up to the exam.

The information and ideas for each poem are separated into four sections.

Context

This section gives background information about the poet. Although you will not be examined on this, it is often helpful and interesting to know more about the poet and, in the case of the literary heritage poets, the times in which they lived.

What happens?

This section tries to sum up the content of the poem. If there are words you have not met before, you may find an explanation of their meaning in the glossary. When you are responding to a poem, remember that there are not many marks for knowing what it is about. Instead you need to use a poem's theme and setting as background for your own opinions.

Structure, language, imagery

These sections help you to explore the poem in more detail, so you can recognise the way poets use their skills. Look back at the poem and see whether you agree with the suggestions and whether you can find more examples of the techniques highlighted in bold. There is an online *Glossary of literary terms*, to which you can refer.

Points to consider

The ideas and questions in this section could really develop your appreciation of the poem. There are often no right or wrong answers to the questions, but considering the ideas in more detail could gain you extra marks for personal interpretation regarding poets' opinions and purposes.

Comparing poems

The essential skill the examiners expect of you is the ability to compare poems. Don't forget that comparison involves looking for differences as well as similarities. This section gives you information about the exam, advises you on time management and helps you to plan your response to make sure you compare throughout.

Tackling the assessments

This section tells you what to do when the exam starts and why it is important to use your time wisely. There is advice on choosing the question, writing a quick plan, how to start your response, using PEE to achieve high marks, examples of responses at grade C and A*, and practice questions for foundation and higher tiers.

A reminder

When writing about the poems, use this guide as a springboard to develop your own ideas. Remember: the examiners are not looking for set responses. You should not read this guide in order to memorise chunks of it, ready to regurgitate in the exam. Identical answers are dull. The examiners hope to reward you for perceptive thought, individual appreciation and varying interpretations. They want to sense you have explored the poems, engaged with the ideas and enjoyed this part of your literature course.

Timelines

Although you will not be asked about a poet's life in the exam, an understanding of what it was like to be living when the poem was written should give you insight into the poet's purpose, language and feelings.

Conflict

Literary heritage poets

Poet	Poem	Year
Alfred Lord Tennyson, 1809–1892	'The charge of the Light Brigade', 1854	1850
Wilfred Owen, 1893–1918	'Futility', 1918	
Margaret Postgate Cole, 1893–1980	'The falling leaves', 1915	1900
e e cummings, 1894–1962	'next to of course god america', 1926	
Stevie Smith, 1902–1971	'Come on, come back', 1957	
Ted Hughes, 1930–1998	'Bayonet charge', 1957	1950
	'Hawk roosting', 1960	

Contemporary poets

Poet	Poem	Year
Ciaran Carson, 1948–	'Belfast confetti'	
John Agard, 1949–	'Flag'	
Robert Minhinnick, 1952–	'The yellow palm'	
Imtiaz Dharker, 1954–	'The right word'	2000
Jane Weir, 1963–	'Poppies'	
Simon Armitage, 1963–	'Out of the blue'	
Choman Hardi, 1974–	'At the border, 1979'	
Owen Sheers, 1974–	'Mametz Wood'	

Relationships

Literary heritage poets

Poet	Poem	Year
William Shakespeare , 1564–1616	'Sonnet 116', 1609	1600
Andrew Marvell, 1624–1678	"To his coy mistress', c. 1660	1650
Elizabeth Barrett Browning, 1806–1861	'Sonnet 43', 1845	1800
Christina Rossetti , 1830–1894	'Sister Maude', 1862	1850
Charlotte Mew , 1869–1928	'The farmer's bride', 1916	1900
Vernon Scannell , 1922–2007	'Nettles', 1950	1950
Phillip Larkin , 1922–1986	'Born yesterday', 1954	

Contemporary poets

Poet	Poem	Year
Mimi Khalvati, 1944–	'Ghazal', 2007	2000
James Fenton, 1949–	'In Paris with you', 1982	
Grace Nichols, 1950–	'Praise song for my mother', 1984	
Carol Ann Duffy, 1955–	'Hour', 2006 'Quickdraw', 2006	
Simon Armitage, 1963–	'Harmonium', 2009 'The manhunt', 2007	
Andrew Forster, 1964–	'Brothers', 2007	

Poem by poem

- What is the context of the poem?
- What happens in the poem?
- How is the poem structured?
- How does the poet use language?
- What imagery does the poet use?

Conflict

Contemporary poems

'At the border, 1979' by Choman Hardi

Context

Choman Hardi was born in Iraqi Kurdistan in 1974, but her family fled to Iran while she was still a baby. When she was five years old, Saddam Hussein became president of the Iraqi Republic and she returned with her family to the country of her birth. At the age of 14, however, the Kurds in Iraq were attacked with chemical weapons. There were mass killings and disappearances and once again Hardi's family was forced into exile.

She settled in England when she was 20 and, although she first wrote her poems in Kurdish, she now writes in English. 'At the border, 1979' is one of the poems in her first collection in English, named *Life for Us*, published in 2004, that explores the terror, violence and persecution of war, alongside the pain of displacement.

What happens?

The poet describes how, at the age of five, she and her family crossed back into Iraq, the country where she had been born. She remembers her sister's naive playful attitude, the sternness of the border guards, the mothers being very emotional because they could return home, and one man's display of affection for his homeland. Since she was so young, she could not understand why a 'thick iron chain' (l. 5) should make any difference between two countries that looked identical to her: the soil 'continued on the other side' (l. 20), it was raining on both sides of the chain, and the same Kurdistan mountains surrounded them. Yet the adults were behaving as though something important was happening.

> **Glossary**
>
> **check-in point (l. 1)**
> a place where official documents are checked
>
> **landscape (l. 13)**
> the appearance of the land
>
> **inhale (l. 16)**
> to breathe in
>
> **encompassed (l. 27)**
> surrounded, enclosed

Kurdish refugees in the mountains of northern Iraq

Structure

Key quotation

The land under our feet continued,

divided by a thick iron chain.

The poem is written in free verse, in seven stanzas of varying lengths. This makes the poem sound conversational, as if Hardi is telling somebody about her experiences at a later date. The second stanza is the shortest and seems to deliver the poet's key message: geographically the landscape is identical; politically there are dangerous differences for Kurdish people.

Most of the lines are end-stopped, i.e. there is a pause and a punctuaion mark at the end of each line, giving the impression that the information in each line is self contained.

Language

The poem is **autobiographical,** written from Hardi's own experience, and the poet directly quotes what people say. It begins with an exclamation: 'It is your last check-in point in this country!' (l. 1) Who is saying this? A parent, another adult or perhaps one of the border guards? Hardi's sister speaks playfully, the mother tells the children they are 'going home' (l. 11) and somebody says 'I can inhale home' (l. 16). This **direct speech** gives the poem **immediacy** and we can easily share in the experience.

Pause for thought

Why do you think the poet speaks in such a choppy way? Does it sound as though lots of memories are flooding into her head? Does it slow the poem down?

Throughout the poem Hardi seems to be questioning what is the same and what is different. This emphasises the young child's lack of understanding.

- 'Soon everything would taste different', she says. Taste can mean more than flavour on the tongue. It is an ambiguous word that can also mean to experience something, suggesting that the family's life is going to change in many ways. Hardi's sister straddles the dividing chain and jokes, but perhaps Hardi, sensing life is going to change dramatically, feels apprehensive at this border point.

● The differences sound exciting when the mother explains how Iraq is 'more beautiful' (l. 13). She repeats the word 'much': 'the roads are much cleaner', 'and people are much kinder'. Can you think of two reasons why she might say this? In contrast the young Hardi comments that the soil is 'the same colour, the same texture'. The repetition of the word 'same' reinforces the puzzlement of the child, who has been told that life will be so much better.

The language used is simple and uncomplicated. Hardi says:

> Writing in a second language is also a form of distancing. Nostalgia is very difficult in poetry: strong emotions can really turn people off. It's important to have a bit of distance in time and space, and using another language will allow you to write about it a bit more neutrally.

> At an event organised by Poet in the City and Amnesty International, 2005 (see www.opendemocracy.net/arts-Literature/exiledpoets_3035.jsp)

Imagery

There are, however, some individual words used **metaphorically** that evoke strong emotions. The word 'inhale' for instance, suggests that the refugee is trying to breathe in all the pleasures and memories of a former life as he or she returns to the homeland. Do you think the word 'encompassed' (l. 27) is a better choice than 'surrounded' would be? Link your answer to the poet's feelings.

The word 'chain' is used four times in the poem, so it must be an important idea. 'Chain' can have different meanings. It can bind together in the way that the links are connected; it can tie you up and confine you; it is even a collective noun for a mountain range. All three concepts are used by Hardi in lines 5, 22, 25 and 27. The Kurds are linked by identity, repressed wherever they live or to wherever they flee, and Kurdistan is a mountainous area.

Ideas to consider

Do you think Hardi is making a point in the last line? Now that she is an adult, how do you think she feels about the way the Kurds were treated by Iraq and Iran? Who does she mean by 'all of us'?

'Belfast confetti' by Ciaran Carson

Context

Ciaran Carson was born in Belfast, the capital city of Northern Ireland, in 1948. He graduated from Queen's University, Belfast, and worked for

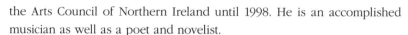

the Arts Council of Northern Ireland until 1998. He is an accomplished musician as well as a poet and novelist.

Carson was a young man in Belfast when the Troubles began in 1969. 'The Troubles' refers to almost 30 years of violence between the nationalists (mainly Roman Catholic) who wanted independence from the UK and the unionists (mainly Protestants) who believed in strengthening the political ties between Northern Ireland and Britain. Armed paramilitary groups, including the Provisional Irish Republican Army (IRA), made Belfast a terrifying place to live between 1969 and 1997 and much of the violence took place around the Protestant Shankill Road and Catholic Falls Road areas. The British government claimed that its forces were in Northern Ireland to keep law and order, but Irish republicans objected strongly to the presence of the British soldiers.

Glossary

'Belfast confetti' (title) the name given to objects and rubble hurled by rioters

fount (l. 3) fountain

asterisk (l. 5) a star-shaped mark (*)

hyphen (l. 5) a short stroke joining two words (-)

labyrinth (l. 11) a maze, a tangle of intricate connections

Balaclava, Raglan, Inkerman, Odessa (ll. 11, 12) famous historical battles

Crimea (l. 13) the scene of the Crimean War (1853–56)

Saracen (l. 15) military tank vehicle

Kremlin (l. 15) the Russian word for fortress; also the government building of the Soviet Union (1922–91)

Makrolon (l. 15) transparent tough material, resistant to impact

walkie-talkies (ll. 15/16) hand-held two-way radio receivers

fusillade (l. 18) rapid continual discharge of firearms

What happens?

Key quotation

I know this labyrinth so well

The poem is written in the first person, giving a dramatic description of what it felt like to be caught up in the violent riots in Belfast in the 1970s. In the aftermath of an IRA bomb, there is chaos and the 'riot squad' moves in. In his confusion and terror the poet cannot find his way through the maze of Belfast streets that he usually knows so well. He is stopped and interrogated by British soldiers, but is unable to communicate with them to answer their straightforward questions. Nothing makes sense to him anymore.

Structure

Carson chooses two stanzas of equal length. The first is in the past tense, describing the violence and its effect when caught up in the conflict. The second stanza shifts suddenly into the present tense. It is as though the narrator is suddenly back inside the experience, reliving the fear of no longer recognising his home town and being questioned by hostile-looking soldiers.

Just as he feels out of control, so the sentences are erratic. His language stops and starts, whether because of 'a burst of rapid fire...' or because he repeatedly loses his way and has to turn back: 'Dead end again.'

Regular use of **enjambement** effectively throws **emphasis** on single words like 'explosion' (l. 4) and 'stuttering' (l. 8) and the natural break at the end of line 16, where he seems to break mid question, stresses his confused state when inhuman masked figures impede his progress.

Language

'Belfast confetti' is a **euphemism** for miscellaneous objects that were thrown during street riots: 'nuts, bolts, nails, car keys', even tin cans. Sometimes they were added to IRA bombs to cause more injury. It is ironic that nuts and bolts, which usually hold things together, should be used in conflict to hurt and alienate others. Also confetti (small pieces of coloured paper) is usually thrown over a new bride and groom to celebrate a happy union but here small pieces of metal are hurled to break up relationships and create discord.

Carson contrasts the short jerky sentences with **lists**, which give a feeling of panic.

The British soldiers in their riot gear seem particularly menacing when he comes face to face with them. With their armoured vehicle, barbed-wire fences and face-shields, they do not even seem human.

The questions on line 17 at the end of the poem are in list form, not only to suggest confusion, but they also inform us of the standard impersonal questions the soldiers ask. The disturbed individual, lost in his own city, seems unable to answer. Do you think the questions also suggest that there are no easy answers to preventing the violence in Belfast?

Punctuation is the way we make sense of language. It tells us when to pause, stop and start again. Too little punctuation causes confusion and too much results in short

> **Grade *booster***
>
> The street names in list format (l. 11) — Balaclava, Raglan, Inkerman, Odessa — follow one after the other. Make the point that the street names themselves are the names of famous battles. You could improve your response by explaining how this reinforces the feeling of relentless conflict.

> **Pause for thought**
>
> Think about 'walkie-talkies'. How does this description add to the effect? Can you link this idea with Carson's concerns about language and communication?

> ***Key quotation***
>
> **every move is punctuated**

chaotic, panicky sentences. The speaker in the poem is caught up in a violent bout of street fighting and cannot 'complete a sentence in his head'. Carson skilfully weaves most types of punctuation mark into the poem.

He even plays **visual tricks**:

- 'Fount' is another word for 'fountain' — 'A fount of broken type' (l. 3) suggests that words are being cut short as the 'confetti' sprays through the air. There is no time for talking, for reasoning.
- 'A burst of rapid fire' is followed by … (an ellipsis), a punctuation mark when there has been something missed out or there's more to follow. What does the reader imagine happens at this point?
- 'An asterisk' on the map (*) looks as though there has been an explosion on paper.
- 'This hyphenated line'. Spot the dash (l. 5), which looks like a hyphen and links the explosion to the asterisk.

Imagery

The whole poem seems to be an **extended metaphor** for the way that violent conflict destroys language. Language is a system of communicating ideas, thoughts and feelings with other people. Take away language and conflict cannot be resolved.

- 'Raining exclamation marks' suggests the sudden shouts and cries of alarm caused by the attack.
- 'An asterisk on the map' (*) looks as though there has been an explosion on paper.
- 'Stuttering' is also used metaphorically to give the sound of 'the burst of rapid fire' as well as the implication that the narrator cannot get his words out coherently.
- All the alleyways and side streets are 'blocked with stops' in the same way that full stops halt the reader.
- 'Fusillade' usually means that a weapon is firing one shot after another: 'A fusillade of question marks' has the effect of one question being fired after another as the narrator struggles to answer in his uncertainty and fear.

Ideas to consider

- A peace deal for Northern Ireland was reached in 1998 after nearly two years of talks and 30 years of conflict. Do you think Carson believes in talking to avoid conflict?
- Do you feel this poem is autobiographical? Pick out lines to support your answer.

12

'Flag' by John Agard

Context

John Agard was born on 21 June 1949 in Guyana (a British colony at the time), on the coast of north-east South America. Guyana gained independence from the UK in 1966, the year before Agard moved to London. He is a poet, playwright and children's author, who often writes about issues of identity and racial conflict. He is well known for his eccentric and lively poetry readings, his poems benefitting greatly from being performed by their author. He lives and works in Sussex.

Study the dictionary definitions in the following glossary. Do you think Agard would add more ideas to these definitions?

What happens?

Agard questions why people are so patriotic. The flag is a symbol of allegiance to one's country and he wonders why it has such power over the decisions people make.

Structure

The poem has five three-line stanzas of equal shape — the shorter middle line and two longer lines giving the appearance of flags 'fluttering in a breeze'.

The first and last lines rhyme in verses 1 and 3, and half-rhyme with long vowel sounds 'o' (ll. 4, 6) and 'ee' (ll. 10, 12) in verses 2 and 4. Then the rhyming pattern changes in the last verse, where 'cloth' (previously at the end of the second line in each verse) sits at the end of the first line, leaving the last two lines as a rhyming couplet. The last two lines sum up the poet's feelings about patriotism.

Agard feels that 'blind patriotism' can make people do what they would personally believe to be morally wrong. Instead of letting their conscience guide them, they support their country and its government at all times. The strong rhyming couplet at the end emphasises Agard's dislike of patriotism, when there is the conviction that one's own country is superior to all others and therefore must always be in the right.

Language and imagery

Each stanza begins with a **question** and goes on to give the poet's answer. There's no sense at any time that somebody else is asking the question. The format allows Agard to put his opinions across in a stronger way.

> ### Glossary
>
> **flag (title)**
> a piece of fabric, usually rectangular, of distinctive colour and design, often flown from a mast or a pole and used to symbolise a country
>
> **patriotism**
> love of country and willingness to sacrifice for it

> ### *Key quotation*
>
> **Blind your conscience to the end.**

The sustained letter 'f' — 'fluttering' (l. 1), 'unfurling' (l. 4), 'flying' (l. 10) — gives the impression of a flag's movements.

Alliteration is used regularly to express growing disgust in the power of a national flag:

> It's just a piece of cloth
> that brings a nation to its knees.

- This line can be interpreted in different ways: literally to kneel before a flag would mean to show respect, to worship what the flag represents. But the expression 'to bring to its knees' means to force someone into submission or cause someone to beg for mercy.

> that makes the guts of men grow bold

- The repeated 'g' sound, formed in the throat (guttural), pushes out his argument.

> that will outlive the blood you bleed

- This repeats the plosive 'bl' sound. Agard adds the word 'blind' in the last line to reinforce his message that 'blind' patriotism is wrong and that many young lives are lost fighting for causes in which its victims may not always believe.

'It's just a piece of cloth' is repeated as a chorus. The throwaway line contrasts with the serious effects of violent war. The poet argues that allegiance to one's country results in false courage and death.

The metaphor 'blind your conscience' suggests a refusal to see what is right. The word 'blind' is similar to 'bind', which would mean the opposite.

Flag waving at a National Front march

Ideas to consider

- In 1916 the British government felt it necessary to introduce military conscription, because reliance on men to join up voluntarily could not keep pace with the ever-increasing casualties of the First World War. Those who had a 'conscientious objection to bearing arms' were freed from military service, but they had to plead their reasons in a tribunal and life was made very difficult for 'conscies', who were either against war in general (pacifists), or did not believe the government of Germany to be their enemy, or would not fight for religious reasons. Do you think Agard would be a conscientious objector?

● People often wave flags because they are proud supporters. Can you think of any occasions when you have waved the flag? Are there occasions when you disagree with the Union Jack being waved?

Flag wavers at a Proms concert in the Royal Albert Hall

'Mametz Wood' by Owen Sheers

Context

Owen Sheers was born in Fiji in 1974, but grew up in Abergavenny, South Wales. He attended King Henry VIII Comprehensive School and then went on to New College, Oxford. As well as a poet, he is a novelist and playwright. 'Mametz Wood' is in his second collection of poetry, *Skirrid Hill*.

The battle to capture Mametz Wood, in Northern France, during the First Battle of the Somme, took place between 5 and 12 July 1916. The wood was eventually captured from the German front line, but the Welsh battalions suffered heavy casualties: 4,000 men died or were wounded. The Royal Welsh Fusiliers, particularly those in the 38th Welsh Division, fought extremely bravely through dense woodland — conditions for which they had had no training. Today a memorial to their courage can be seen, of a red Welsh dragon tearing at barbed wire.

Sheers was visiting the area of Mametz Wood when he was shown a photograph of a grave that had recently been unearthed. He says that the image burned into his mind and he knew he would have to write a poem about it.

Glossary

chit (l. 4) a small piece of paper

relic (l. 5) an object associated with the past, with a saint or remains of a corpse

mimicked (l. 7) copied

flint (l. 7) very hard stone

sentinel (l. 10) guard, sentry

mosaic (l. 14) a design made of small pieces of coloured stone or glass

dance-macabre (l. 15) dance of death; a medieval dance in which a skeleton leads others to their graves

socketed (l. 17) hollowed out

The Welsh at Mametz Wood by Christopher Williams (d. 1934)

Key quotation

their skeletons paused mid dance-macabre

What happens?

For many years farmers have ploughed up bones from soldiers buried in a field near Mametz Wood. On one particular day a grave is discovered where 20 soldiers have been buried. The skeletons still reveal their arms linked together, as though dancing.

Structure

The 21 lines of the poem, although in one long stanza, divide into four sections.

- The first nine lines describe how the farmers have been unearthing pieces of bone for many years.
- The next three lines (ll. 10–12) could stand alone.

  And even now the earth stands sentinel,
  reaching back into itself for reminders of what happened
  like a wound working a foreign body to the surface of the skin.

  The poet's voice is heard here, reflecting on the way discoveries are still being made that bring the past into the present. These three lines introduce the new discovery of the shared grave, which is described in the next six lines.

- The final three lines reintroduce Sheers' feelings about the waste of young vigorous life that is the result of war. He finishes the poem with the observation that 'only now', when dug up after many years, do the 20 'wasted young' get the chance to complain about the way their lives were sacrificed.

Although in free verse, there are two examples of half-rhyme in the poem. Lines 8 and 9 close the first section, almost like a rhyming couplet (run, guns) and lines 19 and 21 end with 'sung' and 'tongues' to give a feeling of finality to the poem.

Language

Sheers' use of **emotive words and phrases** demonstrates his feelings about the futility of war. The dead are 'wasted young' and their 'absent tongues' suggests that they can't speak for themselves.

The description is very **visual**. Lines 14–16 describe the way the skeletons seem to be linking arms in a dance, and line 16 is a poignant reminder that once they were alive and wearing the boots to trudge through the mud, the fields and the forests. It is particularly ironic that the boots have outlived the wearers. Even the empty skulls — 'their socketed heads' — are 'tilted back at an angle/and their jaws...dropped open'. We can see the photo in our minds in all its distressing detail.

Imagery

Sheers describes the fragments of bone in moving **metaphors**:

- 'the china plate of a shoulder blade' (l. 4) makes the piece of bone sound delicate and precious
- 'the relic of a finger' (l. 5) — although 'relic' can mean anything left when the rest has decayed, it also refers to something belonging to a saint, and is considered holy
- 'the blown/and broken bird's egg of a skull' (ll. 5, 6) gives a fragile picture of the empty remains of a young man's head
- 'nesting machine guns' (l. 9) continues the bird image. The collective noun for a group of machine guns, hidden from view, is a 'nest'. What other ideas about the machine guns does the word 'nesting' give?
- 'a broken mosaic of bone' (l. 14) makes a design of the skeletons linked together; they fit together like a jigsaw; the whole picture tells a very different story from that of the individual pieces. Why is the mosaic 'broken'?

The **simile** describing the earth 'like a wound working a foreign body to the surface of the skin' (l. 2) is very effective. Think about the way a splinter is eventually pushed out of your skin. The words 'foreign body' are cleverly ambiguous, not only describing something introduced from the outside, but also referring to the Welsh soldiers who have died while fighting on foreign soil. The French soil is **personified**. Recognising its English or Welsh occupants, it seems to have slowly lifted the skeletons upwards so they can be discovered in peacetime. Sheers seems to have great respect for the earth, which on line 10 'stands sentinel' as though it is keeping watch over its dead.

Ideas to consider

British soldiers always sang to keep their spirits up, whenever they travelled long distances or wanted to think of home. They sang 'Oh! Oh! Oh! What a lovely war!', 'When this lousy war is over, O how happy I shall be', 'Take me back to dear old Blighty' and 'Pack up your troubles in your ol' kit bag'. Do you think, if they could sing now, they might change the words?

Extract from 'Out of the blue' by Simon Armitage

Context

Attack on the twin towers

Simon Armitage was born in Huddersfield, Yorkshire in 1963. He studied geography at Portsmouth Polytechnic, then worked with young offenders. He gained a postgraduate qualification in social work at Manchester University and worked as a probation officer in Oldham until 1994. He has published nine books of poetry and also writes for radio, television and film. He works as a senior lecturer at Manchester Metropolitan University.

'Out of the blue' (2008) consists of three pieces written in response to the anniversaries of three conflicts: a film-poem about 9/11; a piece commissioned by Channel 5 for VE Day; and a radio poem on Cambodia 30 years after the rise of the Khmer Rouge. Broadcast five years after the 9/11 attacks on the USA, 'Out of the blue' won the 2006 Royal Society documentary award.

What happens?

The poem is told from the point of view of a fictional British trader trapped in the north tower of the World Trade Centre, New York, as the planes strike and the horrific events of the day unfold. There is very little political comment. 'For this new poem I was interested much more in bereavement. I also wanted it to reflect what was happening that day inside the towers. To give those inside a voice', Armitage explains. The actor, Rufus Sewell, reads the poem against a backdrop of a dealing office, actual footage of the day itself and some memories from victims' families.

The first stanza describes the distressing image of a figure at the top of the burning tower waving a white shirt in order to be noticed. For the reader, as for the people looking up from the ground below, it is distressingly clear that rescue will be impossible since the tower beneath the waving figure is ablaze.

Structure

The whole poem is 878 lines long, the eight four-line stanzas in the AQA anthology being just an extract. The lines vary in length with regular use of **enjambement** to give a conversational feel, as the trader speaks to his absent loved one, in a desperate bid to share and describe his terrifying situation.

The first five stanzas have the second and fourth lines **rhyming**, always with an action verb in the present tense ending in '-ing'. The tone of the words grows increasingly more desperate, from 'burning', 'turning', 'waving' through 'diving' and 'falling' to hope draining away. The last stanza uses two rhyming couplets, ending with 'sagging' and 'flagging' to stress the hopelessness of the situation.

Language and imagery

- Armitage uses frequent repetition of words to emphasise the horror of the traumatic experience for the first-person narrator. 'Waving, waving' and 'watching, watching' make minutes seem like hours and 'appalling. Appalling' is all that can be said or thought when human bodies drop past. The list: 'wind-milling, wheeling, spiralling, falling' might sound attractive if describing the flight of birds or light aircraft, but the realisation that this describes fellow workers in the building, hurtling away from the heat to their deaths, is almost unbearable. Few people were able to watch newsreel of these horrific images after 9/11.

- Examples of alliteration add to the horror: 'building burning'; 'a soul worth saving'; 'My arm is numb and my nerves are sagging'; 'failing, flagging'.

> **Key quotation**
>
> **Does anyone see
> A soul worth saving?**

- The poet relies on words with long vowel sounds to give the impression of repeated actions and the length of agonised waiting — waving, flying, spiralling, falling, breathing.

- 'here in the gills/I am still breathing' gives a frightening picture of somebody being overcome by smoke, taking his last few breaths, like a fish pulled out of water and gasping weakly.

- The poem tells a story as events are described dramatically as the 'I' gives visual detail to 'you' and in so doing creates images for the reader: the 'white cotton shirt is twirling'; 'I am waving, waving./ Small in the clouds'.

- 'Do you see me, my love.' he asks at the end. 'I am failing, flagging.' The two words 'my love' remind the reader that most of the victims of 9/11 had loved ones they were trying to contact when they realised they would probably not survive. The events of this terrible day are still recent

> **Key quotation**
>
> **I am failing,
> flagging**

and this is one reason why the poem is so hauntingly evocative. 'Flagging' is clever use of **ambiguity** as an exhausted man tries to catch the attention of the rescue services.

Ideas to consider

This is only an extract of a much longer poem. Do you think it is still effective as seven stand-alone stanzas?

The word 'believing' is repeated on a line of its own. Why do you think Armitage chose to do this? Search on the internet for a film of this poem and look at the expressions on the faces of those in the street as they looked up at the burning towers. Their complete incredulity should help your response.

'Poppies' by Jane Weir

Context

Jane Weir was born in Salford in 1963, grew up in Manchester and spent several years in Belfast, before returning to England. She presently lives with her family in Matlock, Derbyshire. As well as writing poetry, she is the fiction editor of *Iota* poetry magazine and runs her own textile and design business. Drawing on her own poems and practice as a designer, she explores the language of textiles in her work.

Jane's first collection of poetry *The Way I Dressed during the Revolution* (Templar Poetry, 2005) was shortlisted for a new writers' award in 2006. Her second collection, *Before Playing Romeo*, was published in 2007. Her work is also published elsewhere in poetry magazines and anthologies, but 'Poppies' was her first poem to be published in a national newspaper.

The poem was commissioned by Carol Ann Duffy for the *Guardian* (July 2009) to be part of a collection of war poetry called *Exit Wounds*. Since its publication, Jane Weir has been contacted by mothers of soldiers from Europe and the USA. She says: 'I wrote the piece from a woman's perspective, which is quite rare, as most poets who write about war have been men. As the mother of two teenage boys I tried to put across how I might feel if they were fighting in a war zone.'

Glossary

Armistice Sunday (l. 1) in the UK, the Sunday closest to Armistice Day (11 November), the anniversary of the end of the hostilities of the First World War at 11 a.m. in 1918

crimped (l. 4) pressed into folds; describes the waviness given to materials by weaving, knitting, plaiting, or other processes

blockade (l. 5) obstacle or obstruction

bias binding (l. 6) a strip of edging material, often used for decoration

blackthorn (l. 16) a spiky shrub

What happens?

In the days before Armistice Sunday, a mother grieves for the loss of her soldier son. She reflects on a time when she had pinned a poppy on her growing son's lapel before he dashed out of the house, enthusiastic for school or conflict and all the excitements that the world had to offer. She finds herself drawn to the war memorial in the churchyard and longs to hear her dead son's voice again.

Structure

The poem is written in free verse, which captures the continuing thoughts of the mother as they crowd her mind through her grieving process. She seems to be internalising her thoughts, while addressing her absent son.

There are four stanzas of differing lengths, two and three being effectively linked by **enjambement**, which creates a pause before 'slowly melting' into stanza four:

> …All my words
> flattened, rolled, turned into felt,
> slowly melting.

Read this section of the poem again to appreciate the pause. Jane Weir explains 'the felt merges and melts, and if one is to grieve one has to, at some point, allow this to dissolve' (AQA GCSE English, 2010 Ready Conference). Do you think the mother is breaking up as she enters her son's empty bedroom? Perhaps the layers of grief over time have deadened her feelings. Nothing will ever be the same again, but the mother has to continue living. Ask yourself, how does the process of loss, yearning and grieving change over time?

Examine the opening of the poem, which begins like a story: 'Three days before…' and the poignant ending where the mother leans against the war memorial, her memories once again raw as she yearns to hear that happy voice from the past, when her son was young, carefree and in love with life.

Key quotation

…I listened, hoping to hear

your playground voice catching on the wind.

Language and imagery

The dramatic monologue seems to be a **lament** (or elegy), where the mother's memory takes her on a journey. The idea of the poppy, a **symbol** of remembrance for the war dead, reminds her of the time she pinned a poppy on her son's blazer. She experiences feelings of loss when she visits her son's empty bedroom. Here time blurs — not only would she have missed her

Pause for thought

Why has Jane Weir used the dove in her poem? For thousands of years the white dove has been a symbol of peace, hope and love. To early Greeks and Romans the dove also represented the love and devotion that comes with caring for a family. The Bible story of Noah's Ark tells how the dove returned with the olive branch, when the flood receded and God wanted Noah and his family to live in peace. Does the mother in the poem yearn for peace?

schoolboy son, leaping 'intoxicated' into his future, but also many times, since his death, she will have visited his room. Do you think the released song bird could also suggest a mother's emotional sense of release once her child has left the house? The narrative moves on to the churchyard, led by another symbol — 'a single dove' — to a war memorial, a record of the sacrifice made by many young men in past conflicts, most of whom would have had grieving mothers.

War is harsh and brutal and many poems are written from the point of view of soldiers and those engaged in war but 'Poppies' looks at the effects of conflict when grief is brought into the home and experienced on the domestic front. The language of maternal caring intermingles with the language of the battlefield:

- The poppy is described with the imagery of conflict. The metaphor, 'spasms of paper red' (l. 5), could denote splatters of blood, perhaps also the sharp, painful agonies of those affected by conflict — soldiers and loved ones alike.
- The bright red poppy contrasts with 'a blockade/of yellow bias binding' (l. 5). The military metaphor perhaps prevents the escape of the raw edge under the binding: the young child has to grow up; the young man is sent into conflict, while still inexperienced.
- A mother checks out her son's school uniform in the way a soldier's kit would be routinely inspected. However, she smooths down the 'shirt's/upturned collar' in a caring way.
- She removes the cat hairs, in the way a female notices detail, the 'sellotape bandaged around (her) hand'. There is a sense of anxiety as the child has to be prepared for the experience of school or the conflicts of the outside world. The cat hairs suggest the marking out of territory — the home, security and ultimately safety — whereas 'bandaged' reinforces the fear of harm, whether from serious injury or everyday knocks. There is a strong sense of the mother wanting to protect and heal.
- Rubbing noses like Eskimos is a common affectionate gesture between parent and child, but the mother knows her son would no longer want such a childish gesture. The word 'graze' instead of the expected 'rub' carries a sense of danger, where a minor scratch could so easily have been a major injury.
- 'Reinforcements of scarf, gloves' (l. 29) would remind any mother of the necessity of warm accessories that a child regularly discounts or loses. 'Reinforcements' also has the connotation of additional personnel or equipment sent to support military action. When the

mother leaves the house to walk to the church yard, she leaves her essential 'kit' behind and sets off to face her own personal battle ahead.

The 'gelled/blackthorns of your hair' is a **metaphorical phrase**, combining the fashionable hairstyle of the young man, now consciously aware of his physical appearance, with the spiky hedgerow. The youth would also be very reluctant to allow his mother to demonstrate her affection. Sharp wounding thorns are in direct contact with maternal tenderness. Perhaps it is the poignant memory of the words purposely left unsaid, minor battles of adolescence, that drag up the layered grief again.

Compare two **similes** in the poem. The young boy dashes out of the house 'the world overflowing/like a treasure chest' (l. 20), and the bereaved mother leans against the war memorial 'like a wishbone' (l. 32). A treasure chest holds mystery, excitement and adventure and surely life should be able to offer such delights to a young person. In contrast, the wishbone holds a sense of longing, of wishing the lost son back into existence. The wishbone is joined until snapped apart, just as the bond between mother and son has been physically destroyed.

With her love and knowledge of working with textile design, Jane Weir explains in her talk to teachers (AQA 2010 Ready Conference): 'As a designer I am also aware of the similarities between the "making" of a poem and that of "printing", "weaving" or "stitching".' 'Poppies' has frequent **'textile' images** to explore.

- The petals of the paper poppy are 'crimped' (l. 4), suggesting the ridges or curls in the paper. The crimp is also the name for the number of waves along the length of a wool fibre. 'To crimp', as a military term, means to recruit into the army by coercion or under false pretences. Thousands of young men, particularly in 1914, were persuaded to fight for duty and the glory of their country, not realising the horrors of combat and the high possibility that they would be killed. Their names would probably be traceable on the war memorial in the last stanza.
- 'All my words/flattened, rolled, turned into felt' (l. 17) is the line where the agonies of bereavement, the emotions of an anxious mother sending her son into independence and the process of felt-making seem to come together. Felt is made by layers of wool being compacted together under pressure. Eventually, when water is added, the woollen fibres shrink together — like a melting process. Think about the emotions a parent who loses a son must experience: the build-up of pressure over time, the impenetrable

sadness, the thickening numbness, and the process of dissolving into grief.

- How does your stomach feel when you are upset? Lines 27 and 28 — 'my stomach busy/making tucks, darts, pleats' express in needlework imagery the restless busyness of anxiety.
- 'The dove pulled freely against the sky, an ornamental stitch' (l. 33) is a visual metaphor. Imagine the thread being pulled through material to leave a decorative mark, just like a white bird against the sky. Uniforms also have decoration, sometimes denoting military rank or bravery, sometimes demonstrating a responsibility, like prefect or house captain in the secondary school. Once again memories seem to blur into past and present.

Ideas to consider

With its strong visual qualities the poem weaves its images like a tapestry. How would you illustrate each stanza of the poem? Other tactile references help the reader to experience the mother's emotions: in a particularly poignant image she traces 'the inscriptions on the war memorial'.

Wilfred Owen's mother received news of her son's death on Armistice Day, the day that marked the end of the First World War.

'The right word' by Imtiaz Dharker

Context

Imtiaz Dharker was born in Pakistan in 1954 and grew up in Glasgow. She is a poet, artist and documentary film-maker and now divides her time between London and Mumbai. 'The right word' is from her collection of poetry entitled *Terrorist at my Table*, published in 2006.

What happens?

The poet, writing in the first person, examines the word 'terrorist' from different points of view, moving through other names for people who are involved in violence in order to gain recognition for their cause. 'Are words no more/than waving, wavering flags?' she asks — does the interpretation of a word depend on your country, whether you are waving the patriotic flag, confident in justice and rights, or whether you are unsure ('wavering') about your country's involvement in violent warfare? By the end of the poem she has acknowledged that behind the label 'terrorist' there is somebody's young son, respectful of his country's traditions and welcomed in his own community, but still prepared to fight violently for a cause in which he passionately believes.

Glossary

terrorist (l. 3) someone involved in an organised system of intimidation, usually for political purposes

freedom-fighter (l. 7) someone who fights in an armed movement for the liberation of a nation, etc. from a government considered unjust/tyrannical

militant (l. 10) someone who seeks to advance a cause by violence

guerrilla warrior (l. 15) someone who takes part in warfare by harassing an army in small groups

martyr (l. 18) someone who undergoes death or great suffering in support of a belief, cause or principle

Structure

The poem is written in nine stanzas of unequal length and in free verse. An effective use of rhyme is in stanza seven, where the first and last lines rhyme with the words 'you' and 'too'. 'One word for **you**.' Dharker now decides. The word for 'terrorist' in stanza one has been replaced, in gradual stages. In its place is the word 'boy' — 'a boy who looks like your son, **too**' and the unexpected rhyme shocks with the idea that anybody's son could become passionately involved in an organised system of intimidation for his own political beliefs. Dharker seems to be saying that 'the right word' just depends on where your political sympathies lie.

Pause for thought

The term 'terrorist' carries strong negative connotations and is used as a political label, condemning violence as being unjustified. Those labelled as terrorists by others are unlikely to call themselves by the term. Instead they name themselves freedom fighters, militants, guerrillas, vigilantes, liberators, revolutionaries, rebels. Each party in a conflict would probably describe its opponents as terrorists.

Instead of providing a glossary for this poem it is interesting to compare how a dictionary defines the words. Dharker is trying to find 'the right word'. Which word would you use?

Language and imagery

Dharker relies heavily on **repetition** to get her point across:

- She plays with the first line 'Outside the door' throughout the poem. A door is a means of access; metaphorically, it is a barrier. In the first stanza she is afraid of the terrorist 'lurking' ominously. The door then becomes 'that door' and in stanza four 'your door'. She gradually brings the reader into her dilemma, inviting us to question what is 'the right word'. The word 'outside' is repeated in the first seven stanzas, but 'I open the door' in stanza eight allows the boy to come in from outside, to enter.
- 'Shadows', suggesting a dark area where fears and doubts hide, is also repeated in the first six stanzas. We are frightened of terrorist acts in our own country, suspecting anybody who carries a rucksack

Key quotation

Are words no more than waving, wavering flags?

on the Underground or leaves a suitcase on a station platform. But it is only a 'boy' (still a very young man) who is left when the shadows disappear. He has to be invited in, where (to his mother) he becomes 'the child'.

- 'too hard' and 'too steady' are descriptions of somebody confident and unwavering in his convictions. They are uncomfortable descriptions for a mother to give to her son.

'Is that the wrong description?' the poet asks, drawing the reader into the poem, and 'I haven't got this right' gives an **air of immediacy.** She insists that we think carefully about our easy use of the word 'terrorist' when she writes 'outside **your** door' (l. 13) and 'a boy who looks like **your** son, too' (l. 28).

Ideas to consider

Despite the irregular structure, stanzas one and nine have the same three-line format, but the description and mood gradually change until they bear little resemblance. A terrifying unknown 'terrorist' becomes a loved child, respectfully entering his home to eat with his family. Trace the way the name of the 'terrorist' changes through the stanzas to see how she does this.

Some groups, when involved in a struggle for what they believe to be freedom from oppression in their own country, have been called 'terrorists' by Western governments or the media. Later, these same individuals, having become leaders of their liberated nations, are called 'statesmen' by similar organisations. Two examples of this are the Nobel peace prize winners Menachem Begin and Nelson Mandela. Read their biographies to understand how and why this happened.

'The yellow palm' by Robert Minhinnick

Context

Robert Minhinnick was born in 1952 in Neath, South Wales. He studied at the universities of Aberystwyth and Cardiff, then, after working in an environmental field, co-founded Friends of the Earth (Cymru).

As well as being an active environmental campaigner, he is an essayist, novelist and poet. He now lives in Porthcawl, South Wales. His eighth collection of poetry, *King Driftwood* (Carcanet Press, 2008), displays his keen awareness of both climate change and the current situation in the Middle East.

What happens?

The poem describes Minhinnick's experiences when he was walking through Baghdad in 1998. The bombing of Iraq (code-named Operation Desert Fox) was a major four-day bombing campaign on Iraqi targets from 16–19 December 1998, by the USA and UK.

'I'm inspired by beauty and I'm inspired by fear and they often go together', Minhinnick explains. 'I think I was inspired to write about Iraq and the USA because they're both beautiful places, but filled now with fearful things that scare you cold, deadly things. '

Structure

Six stanzas of six lines each are written in ballad form using iambic and anapaest metre. The first line is repeated at the beginning of each stanza to suggest a series of experiences following one after another and the final line of each stanza is usually in three strong iamb feet — 'that **knows**/no **ar**/mi **stice**', with two cases where an anapaest metre (triple foot) precedes the last two iambs — 'in the **Mo**/ther **of** /all **Wars**'. This metric pattern is used throughout in lines 2 and 4 also. The simplicity of this metre, with lines 2, 4 and 6 rhyming throughout, gives a song-type rhythm, which contrasts with the seriousness of the content.

Language and imagery

- Each stanza also contains a contrast in mood. Beauty conflicts with violence and the result is disturbing.
- The 'lilac stems', symbols of early love and mourning, make a pretty picture, but the detail that the dead man has been prematurely and cruelly killed by breathing poison gas distorts the image. Thousands were killed or suffered from horrific diseases or birth defects as a result of chemical weapons used by the Iraqi government.
- 'The golden mosque' is a beautiful building built for worship and tranquillity, but an unexpected violent attack has brought the violence of war into the worshippers' daily lives.
- The offering of a small amount of money to two beggars becomes particularly moving when their salutes show they themselves are defeated old soldiers in exile, blinded by war.
- The fresh smell of the Tigris cannot compete with the cruel relentless heat — even the sun is personified in war-related terms: 'barbarian' and 'armistice'.
- The Cruise missile flying slowly across the sky overhead, described metaphorically as a 'caravan', is in stark contrast to the usual procession of carts, mules or camels and would be terrifying to

> **Pause for thought**
>
> 'the muezzin's eyes/were wild with his despair'
>
> Do you feel the poet shares this desperation?

> **Key quotation**
>
> **down on my head fell the barbarian sun**
>
> **that knows no armistice**

Glossary

lilac (l. 3) a pale purple or white fragrant shrub

Palestine Street a busy thoroughfare in Baghdad

mosque (l. 9) a Muslim place of worship

muezzin (l. 11) a man who calls Muslims to prayer

dinars (l. 16) currency in Iraq

Imperial Guard (l. 17) the personal guard force of the Shahs of Iran, active from 1942 to 1979. Later they saw action in the Iran–Iraq War 1980–88

Mother of all Wars (l. 18) In 1991 during the Gulf War, Saddam Hussein threatened the USA that, if it invaded Iraq, there would be 'The Mother of all Wars'

Tigris (l. 20) the river that runs through Baghdad

barbarian (l. 23) fierce, brutal or cruel

armistice (l. 24) a situation in a war where the warring parties agree to stop fighting, so an attempt can be made to negotiate peace

Cruise missile (l. 26) a guided missile that flies to its target close to the Earth's surface

caravan (l. 27) a procession (of wagons or mules or camels) travelling together

salaam (l. 34) a greeting meaning 'peace', used in Islamic countries

witness, knowing the death and destruction it was about to cause. (In the four-day Operation Desert Fox attack on Iraq in December 1998, the USA and its allies used 90 air-launched cruise missiles.) Yet a beggar child's beautiful and innocent smile, even as he looks up at the missile, for a moment transfixes the poet and dispels the horror.

- The palm trees are heavy with ripe fruit and the idea of a beggar child being able to harvest the dates is pleasing. The simile 'sweeter than salaams' echoes the idea of peace, but the final line 'the fruit fell in his arms' uses ambiguous war imagery as a sad reminder of young futile death. (War dead are often referred to as 'the fallen'.) Once again the contrast in mood is disturbing.

- Minhinnick uses colour to make the images more vivid. 'Lilac stems', 'golden mosque' and 'yellow dates' are vibrant colours, but they are quickly dulled by the 'black dinars' and the menacing 'silver caravan'.

- The alliterative 's' sound is used effectively in stanza five, where the Cruise missile's flight, close to the Baghdad streets, is frighteningly described:

> a slow and silver caravan
> on its slow and silver mile. (ll. 27, 28)

PHILIP ALLAN LITERATURE GUIDE FOR GCSE

The sustained 's' sound and repeated word 'slow' make the shiny flying bomb sound dauntingly sinister, yet, when used in the final line of the stanza — 'and ble**ss**ed it with a **s**mile' (l. 30) — the sibilant 's' transforms the sombre mood. Once again fear and beauty co-exist.

Ideas to consider

A ballad is a simple song-like form of poem. Why do you think Minhinnick chose this form?

This poem describes Baghdad in 1998, and, more than a decade later, Iraq is still a war-torn country. In 2003, US and UK troops invaded Iraq to disarm Saddam Hussein of weapons of mass destruction. Evidence that such weapons existed has never been found. The number of deaths caused by the violence may never be known, but it is believed that, in 2009, it already exceeds 1 million. The United Nations agency for refugees estimates that nearly 5 million Iraqis have been displaced since 2003.

Poems from the English literary heritage

'Bayonet charge' by Ted Hughes

Context

Edward James Hughes (Ted) was born in 1930 in Mytholmroyd, West Yorkshire and died in 1998. He wrote his first poems when he was 15 and won a scholarship to Pembroke College, Cambridge, in 1948, to study English. He seemed fascinated by the First World War experiences of his father and uncle, imagining fearful images of trench warfare. While still a child he had also gained an interest in the natural world and the violence required to survive in harsh environments. He was appointed England's Poet Laureate in 1984 and is considered by many to be one of the twentieth century's greatest English poets.

What happens?

A First World War soldier, carrying his heavy rifle, runs terrified across a ploughed field, towards the enemy, who are firing repeatedly from behind a distant hedge. Hughes imagines him questioning his individual role in the war and why he continues to run towards such danger. It is as though he has been frozen in time for a second. Suddenly a hare, caught in the firing, dies violently, and he realises he has to continue forward — not for any of the reasons he had previously believed, such as patriotism and honour — but simply to escape the terror of 'that blue crackling air' and the fate of the hare.

> **Glossary**
>
> **khaki (l. 2)**
> a yellowish-brown sturdy cloth used for British soldiers' uniforms
>
> **footfalls (l. 13)**
> the sounds of footsteps
>
> **statuary (l. 15)**
> statue(s)
>
> **threshing (l. 17)**
> thrashing about
>
> **bayonet (l. 19)**
> a blade fixed onto a rifle

Structure

The poem is written in free verse in three stanzas. The first stanza, eight lines in length, describes the situation. The second stanza, seven lines long, halts for a moment to explore the soldier's 'bewilderment'. The third stanza, again eight lines, describes the dying hare and the soldier's realisation that he has to keep charging forward to stand any chance of survival.

In line 1 the soldier finds himself 'suddenly' in a nightmarish battle scene; by line 23 he is fully awakened to dangerous reality.

British soldiers in the trenches

Language

The soldier's inexperience is emphasised by the **repetition** of 'raw', first left isolated at the end of line one and then in 'raw-seamed' (l. 2), a description of the rough, hastily-made uniform. No amount of training could prepare this youth for the horror of real combat. Another hyphenated word Hughes creates is 'shot-slashed' (l. 15) to provide a concise visual image of the way the ploughed furrows have become a violent war zone.

Alliteration is used occasionally for effect. 'Cold clockwork' (l. 10) relies on the short harsh 'c' sound to suggest the unfeeling sense of fate and 'plunged past' (l. 19) evokes desperation in the heavy plosive 'p'. The most effective example is in the final line 'his terror's touchy dynamite', where the sudden strong **iambic rhythm** throws emphasis on the 't' to suggest the soldier's raw fear exploding within him. Note the difference between 'stumbling' on line 3, which implies some confusion in the nightmarish scenario, and 'plunged' (l. 19) as the need for speed is realised.

Many **verbs** in stanzas one and three are **violent** and active: 'stumbling', 'threshing', 'plunged', 'yelling' — with the use of **onomatopoeia** in 'smacking', 'smashed', 'crackling' to plunge the reader into the soldier's terrifying experience. Stanza two, however, seems to step away from the action to consider the running soldier's thoughts, (or do you think these are the poet's reflections?).

Enjambement is used effectively throughout to give a sense of running, but at the end of line nine 'he almost stopped —' the reader has to pause as well.

Imagery

Hughes uses imagery throughout the poem to express his imagined horror as one individual runs across no-man's land. 'Bullets smacking the belly out of the air' **personifies** the air, which is being viciously attacked by the constant fusillade of enemy rifle fire. We get the feeling that breathing is difficult through fear and gunpowder. And it is the 'blue crackling air' that is igniting his panic in the **metaphor** 'terror's touchy dynamite'.

The poem is full of **similes** to give vivid detail to the reader.

> **Key quotation**
>
> In what cold clockwork of the stars and the nations was he the hand pointing that second?

- The heavy rifle is 'as numb as a smashed arm' — for the moment he can't stop to use it, yet has to 'lug' it with him in case he gets close enough to use the bayonet.
- The soldier had joined the army with 'a patriotic tear' in his eye, believing there was glory and honour in fighting for his country but, alone on the danger of the battlefield he is 'sweating like molten iron from the centre of his chest'. His allegiance to his country was strong and firm, but his conviction is flowing away from him — his heart has only one job left now: to pump blood around his terrified body.
- 'He was running/like a man who has jumped up in the dark' not understanding why he is there or what he is doing.
- In his bewildered state it is as though he freezes to question whether he should continue — 'his foot hung like/statuary in mid-stride'.
- The list of earlier feelings about reasons for going to war, (l. 20) ending with 'etcetera' to suggest that none of them is now important, drops 'like luxuries in a yelling alarm/to get out'. Survival is all that matters now.

Ideas to consider

Look at the way Hughes uses colour in his descriptions. Why do you think he chooses to do this?

The extract below is from a soldier's letter in 1916:

Lieutenant Wallace said, 'We have been ordered to go on at all costs and must comply with this order'. At this he stood up and within a few seconds dropped down riddled with bullets.

Hughes would have heard stories like this, which inspired him in his poetry. He says: 'Imagine what you are writing about. See it and live it' (*Poetry in the Making*).

'Come on, come back' by Stevie Smith

Context

The poet known as Stevie Smith was born in Kingston upon Hull, Yorkshire, in 1902. Her real name was Florence Margaret Smith and she was brought up by a feminist aunt when her mother became ill and her father deserted his family by running off to sea. Common themes in her writing are death, loneliness and war, and human cruelty. A novelist as well as a poet, she never married, and died in 1971.

Glossary
Austerlitz (l. 2) the poet imagines a future battle on an old battleground. It was here in 1805 that Napoleon and his French troops defeated the armies of Russia and Austria
Vaudevue (l. 3) perhaps a French-style name. Similar to Old French 'vaudevire', meaning a light popular song
Memel (l. 7) the German name for a coastal town in Lithuania, seized by Nazi Germany in 1939. By 1941 the Nazis had murdered most of the Jewish population in Hitler's 'final solution'. Smith imagines it as the location of a conference assessing methods of exterminating human beings
M L 5 (l. 9) probably a made-up name for a chemical. 'Come on, come back' was written in the 1950s, and Smith would have known about such things as Cyclone-B, the gas used on the Jews in Nazi death camps
hummock (l. 13) little hill
idiot (l. 19) someone with a severe learning disability (a word no longer used in this sense)

What happens?

The poem describes a dramatic, imaginary event in a future war, involving two characters. A tortured female soldier, her memory and identity erased, throws herself into an icy lake and drowns, pulled down by a fierce undercurrent. An enemy guard, finding her clothes, waits patiently and in vain for her return, while making and then playing a reed pipe. The tune he plays is one known and sung by all soldiers, with its haunting words, 'Come on, come back'. In her own words, Smith says, 'People in rather odd circumstances are what my poems are about.'

Structure

The eight stanzas of the poem are of varying lengths and mostly in free verse. The first stanza rhymes lines 2 and 3 with 'Austerlitz' and 'sits' followed by 'alone' and 'stone' in lines 4 and 5. The rhymes here seem to introduce the setting, like the beginning of a story. Further occasional couplets rhyme in stanzas two, three and eight. 'M L **5**/has left her just **alive**' is shocking in its brevity and 'Favourite of Vaude**vue**/for she had sung it **too**' provides a reminder that soldiers of all armies sing songs to keep their spirits up, often knowing they may never 'come back' to their homeland.

Pause for thought

Napoleon's Proclamation to his Soldiers, 1805:

'In the battle of Austerlitz…you have covered yourselves with eternal glory. An army of one hundred thousand men which was commanded by the emperors of Russia and Austria has been, in less than four hours, either cut off or dispersed. Those that escaped your swords have thrown themselves into the lakes.'

Do you think Smith read this proclamation? How could it link to the poem?

Language and imagery

When Smith read her poems aloud she read slowly and rather monotonously. Read this way the technique of **assonance** is clearer in this poem. Stanza five uses the long 'i' sound in 'mind', 'plight', 'white', 'moonlight', 'icy' and 'dives' for dramatic effect as the fearful girl continues to swim across the black lake. As she is pulled down to the depths the words 'swiftly severing' quicken the pace by the use of short vowel sounds.

Alliteration of sustained letters such as 'm' and 'w' gives a mysterious feeling of time passing — 'At midnight in the moonlight', 'Waiting, whiling away the hour/Whittling', whereas the repeated 's' sound in 'the swift and subtle current's close embrace' has a watery, mysterious, almost whispering, effect.

Words and phrases are often **repeated** for emphasis. 'Alone' (ll. 5, 6) reinforces the damaged girl's loneliness; 'as secret, as profound, as ominous' suggests that her empty, depressed state of mind can be compared to the depths of the treacherous lake. The 'white moonlight', the only way forward in her despair, is repeated using **metaphors** to describe it as a 'ribbon' (l. 23) and a 'river' (l. 30), a long thin stretch of light across 'the icy waters of the adorable lake'.

'Adorable' is an example of the quirky, unexpected selection of vocabulary that jolts the reader of Smith's poetry. Why does she choose a word that means 'lovable and charming in a childlike way' to describe the icy waters of a black lake? Is the girl now reduced to a small child, having had her memory removed? And why the repeated emphasis on 'ominous' to describe the girl's mind? Perhaps she's a danger to herself in her present 'plight'? This **unusual use of vocabulary** offers plenty of scope for analysis.

Ideas to consider

The poem has references to a past battle, yet is set in a future war and written in the present tense. The cruelty, loss and trauma of all wars is an issue here, regardless of location or historical date. Both men and women caught up in conflict question 'Ah me, why am I here?' (l. 12).

One of Smith's regular themes is that of death. 'In my poems the dead often speak,' she says. Do you think the girl soldier welcomes the water's 'amorous embrace'? As she 'sleeps on', can she rest in peace, now she no longer hears the songs of war?

'Futility' by Wilfred Owen

Context

At the time of Wilfred Owen's death in 1918, aged 25, and only seven days before the armistice was declared, he was virtually unknown. It was only after he had been killed in battle and his poems describing his war experiences had been published that he was recognised as one of the great voices of the First World War.

What happens?

The body of a soldier, supposedly killed in battle, lies on the snow. Usually the morning sun can provide warmth and life, but nothing can bring life back to this young man. Owen, in the persona of a shocked comrade, questions why nature creates such miracles, for life to be so senselessly wiped out.

Structure

The poem is written in fourteen lines with some of the features of a traditional **sonnet**, but instead of eight lines followed by six, it is divided into two seven-line stanzas. The kind of tight control required in rhythm and rhyme for a traditional sonnet might not be as appropriate when the voice of the persona is shocked and full of despair. Some irregularity, therefore, is required.

The rhythm becomes more controlled with stronger **iambic metre** (/-) after the first four lines. It is as if the urgency of the moment and the initial faith in the sun's power to revive his fallen friend need a rushed chaotic rhythm, but as soon as the realisation sets in that the sun has no power over death, the rhythm becomes steadier and more sombre.

The fifth and final lines of each stanza **rhyme**: snow/know; tall/all, at points in the poem where his understanding of the situation changes. Elsewhere there are examples of **pararhyme**, a favourite technique of Owen, where the consonant sounds remain the same, but the vowel sound changes: 'sun/sown', 'seeds/sides', 'star/stir', 'tall/toil', 'snow/now'. The sonnet framework is still in place, but the rhymes are not comfortable and complete in places where he questions the fate of his dead comrade.

Language and imagery

Unlike many of Owen's earlier poems there is no horrific detail of violent, agonising deaths to shock the reader. In 'Futility' the **tone** is sad with simple single-syllable words used effectively and the last lines kept shorter to give the effect of a **lament**. Note how commands such as 'Move' and 'Think', (when the speaker is still irrationally trying to revive the dead man), change to questions in the last five lines — unanswered questions, since Owen has no answers for the way war destroys not only human beings, but the whole of creation.

The sun is **personified** throughout. 'Gently its touch awoke him once', combined with 'whispering' and 'kind old sun', form an affectionate image of such a power that gently woke the farm boy back home. At the end of the poem, however, grief turns to bitterness and the sun's attempts are 'fatuous'. In his lack of understanding of why earth's wondrous creations can be destroyed, Owen seems to be questioning whether the sun's power is a beneficial force. It may have brought a dead planet to life, but to what disillusioned end?

'Whispering of fields unsown' is an **ambiguous** clause, suggesting not only the barren fields left behind in England, because of the farmer's absence, but also the future now denied to the young man, who had most of his life before him, but who has become an innocent victim of conflict. 'Was it for this the clay grew tall?' has similar layers of meaning, where clay might remind the reader of creation stories where God makes man out of clay or earth (Adam means 'red earth').

Ideas to consider

'My subject is War, and the pity of War', Owen said. It was only after the First World War that the term 'war poet' came into use. Poets, experiencing the real horrors of conflict, were able to express themselves in their poetry and raise awareness of life and death in the trenches and their lack of faith in their military superiors. Many of the 'war poets', like Owen, died

> ### Pause for thought
>
> 'Are limbs, so dear-achieved, are sides,
>
> Full-nerved — still warm — too hard to stir?'
>
> What do you feel the speaker is doing when the words 'still warm' are separated from the rest of the line?

> ### Key quotation
>
> **O what made fatuous sunbeams toil**
>
> **To break earth's sleep at all?**

> ### Grade *booster*
>
> A word such as 'O' (l. 13) suddenly thrown into speech is called an interjection. Show the examiner that you can appreciate its effect when writing about the mood of the poet and improve the quality of your response. A single sound like this can express so much pain and anguish at the end of the poem. It is as though the speaker has broken down in his distress.

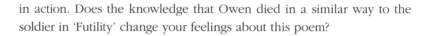

in action. Does the knowledge that Owen died in a similar way to the soldier in 'Futility' change your feelings about this poem?

'Hawk roosting' by Ted Hughes

Context

See Ted Hughes, p. 29.

What happens?

'Hawk roosting' is a dramatic monologue in the voice of a hawk who looks down from the tallest tree in the wood on the whole of 'Creation'. His predatory nature, in its non-human state, is violent and unsentimental. The hawk sees itself as perfection, the highest achievement of creation and is 'going to keep things like this'.

Structure

The poem consists of six four-line stanzas, showing 'no change' (l. 23) as the hawk insists. Lines 3 and 4 are the only rhyming lines, where the short words 'feet' and 'eat' introduce the idea of the hawk as a violent killing machine, right at the beginning of the poem

Language and imagery

Key quotation

Nothing has changed since I began.

My eye has permitted no change.

- The **present tense** gives the poem a timeless feel — the hawk was there at the 'Creation' and 'Nothing has changed since (it) began.'
- The poem begins with 'I' and the **pronouns** 'my', 'me' and 'mine' are regularly repeated to emphasise the conceit and arrogance of the creature. 'No arguments assert my right,' the hawk states. 'I kill where I please because it is all mine.'
- Occasional **repetition** is used. 'My hooked head' and my 'hooked feet' reinforce the killer image, where the beak captures and the feet

perch securely and later carry away the prey. Nature has designed the bird to be suited to its environment in every aspect.

Lines 22–23, each a short confident statement, repeat the word 'change' to stress the bird's proud conviction that perfection does not need adjustment.

- 'My flight is direct/through the bones of the living' uses 'direct' to describe the straight confident path taken by a hawk the instant it spots movement of a living creature. In 'the allotment of death' it believes it has been chosen by God to kill other creatures.

- Throughout the poem the hawk assumes a **God-like image**. It considers itself God's supreme achievement and holds 'Creation in my foot'. As it circles the earth using the 'air's buoyancy', the earth's face is 'upwards for my inspection'. With such power the bird can 'revolve it all slowly'.

> **Key quotation**
>
> **There is no sophistry in my body**
>
> **My manners are tearing off heads**

- Hughes uses a variety of punctuation throughout the poem. Many lines are end-stopped, probably to ensure the self-assured, assertive tone of the hawk is clearly understood. The vocabulary is as direct and brutal as the predator.

Ideas to consider

With which of the following analyses do you agree?
- 'Ted Hughes is trying to show a life-force that is clearly non-human, the wildness and brutality of a creature in its natural state.'
- 'The hawk represents the way power and wealth preys on the weak and poor in this world.'
- 'Because of Hughes' respect for nature, it is highly unlikely that he would use a hawk anthropomorphically to describe humans.'
- 'Using human language, the poet tries to explore how alien the hawk's view of life is to our own.'

'next to of course god america i' by e e cummings

Context

Edward Estlin Cummings was born in Cambridge, Massachusetts, USA on 14 October 1894. In the First World War he was a volunteer ambulance driver, but was imprisoned by the French, on suspicion that he held critical views of France's part in the war. After the war he travelled the world writing poetry (many of them anti-war poems protesting the USA's

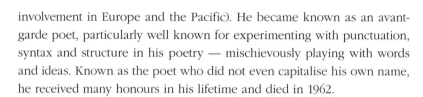

involvement in Europe and the Pacific). He became known as an avant-garde poet, particularly well known for experimenting with punctuation, syntax and structure in his poetry — mischievously playing with words and ideas. Known as the poet who did not even capitalise his own name, he received many honours in his lifetime and died in 1962.

What happens?

The poem seems to begin with Cummings proclaiming his love for his country by quoting words from 'The star-spangled banner,' the American national anthem and another patriotic song, 'My country, 'tis of thee', also known as 'America', and sung to the tune of 'God save the Queen'. But the tone becomes quite obviously cynical as he mocks the way some people, particularly politicians, 'acclaim' America's 'glorious name' and he goes on to focus on the numerous soldiers killed in battle. He argues that they went to war without considering whether it was right — or even dangerous — to do so, and were called heroes when they had been sacrificed for their country's cause. Should nobody speak their mind in this 'land of the free', he asks? Should young men be prepared to rush into any conflict that America engages in? Having expressed his beliefs so passionately, a second voice, who has previously been listening, describes the speaker quickly downing 'a glass of water'.

The star-spangled banner

O say can you see,

by the dawn's early light,

what so proudly we hailed

at the twilight's last gleaming,

whose broad stripes and bright stars,

through the perilous fight,

o'er the ramparts we watched,

were so gallantly streaming?

And the rocket's red glare,

the bombs bursting in air,

gave proof through the night

that our flag was still there.

O say does that star-spangled banner yet wave

o'er the land of the free

and the home of the brave?

America

My country, 'tis of thee,

Sweet land of liberty,

Of thee I sing;

Land where my fathers died,

Land of the pilgrims' pride,

From every mountainside

Let freedom ring!

Structure

The poem is in sonnet form of 14 lines, with the rhyme pattern:

ABAB CDCD EFG FEG

and divides into a 4, 4, 6 sonnet pattern. The final six lines could stand alone as a separate stanza, although Cummings prefers to separate the last line for dramatic effect. The mood changes at line 9 when the emphasis shifts from cynicism to 'the heroic happy dead'. Is Cummings angry now? Or is he very critical? Perhaps he grows slightly hysterical as he protests about the futile waste of 'beautiful' young lives?

The two final triplets have a tight effective rhyme scheme, not like the corny patriotism of the national anthem rhymes, but with emotive words such as 'dead', 'slaughter' and 'mute'.

The metre is irregular for the first eight lines, with lines 6 and 7 changing to iambic pentameter, before the sudden change in line eight in order to mock the slang exclamations used in the 1920s, all probable euphemisms for 'by God!'

> by jingo by gee by gosh by gum

At the start of the final six lines, (l. 9) where Cummings' mood changes from its mockery, the lines once again take up the solemn iambic pentameter rhythm associated with the sonnet form. Only for the last line does it change, where 'rapidly' is inserted after 'drank' instead of before it, creating an unexpected pause after 'drank'. What impression does this give of the drinker's state of mind?

Cummings writes his poem without punctuation, which challenges the reader to work out his/her own interpretation. Some interesting punctuation, however, is included:

- Speech marks illustrate the 13 lines spoken by the main voice of the poem.
- The question mark at the end of line 13 emphasises the strength and conviction of the speaker's protest: he really does want readers to consider his point.
- The full stop after 'He spoke.' (l. 14) contrasts by its simplicity and brevity with the passion of the previous lines.

Language

At which point, when reading the poem, do you begin to suspect Cummings' **sarcasm**? The throwaway expression 'and so forth' suggests he has little respect for any of the lines of the national anthems. He does not complete the lines of the song lyrics: they have nothing important to say.

'deafanddumb' is purposely written as one word. Worldwide, America is praised, he states, and even those who can neither hear nor speak still praise its glorious name. This idea is played on at the end of line 13 with 'mute', which implies a refusal to speak out, not just the inability to speak.

Line 8 uses a list to make its point as well as **alliterative letters**, 'j' and the gushing 'g' sound, with 'glorious' and 'gorry' preceding 'gosh' and 'gum'. 'What of it we should worry' repeats the 'w' sound to question

Grade *booster*

To impress the examiner you could comment on the effective use of enjambement when a pause after 'my' but before 'country' emphasises the patriotic feel of the phrase, and the division of 'beaut-' and 'iful' makes the death of such vibrant youth more poignant with the stress left on the first syllable.

Pause for thought

Can you recognise the ambiguity in the first line, since there is no punctuation between 'god' and 'america'?

America's patriotic fervour. Perhaps the most moving example of alliteration is the **oxymoron** of 'the heroic happy dead'. How can the dead be happy? Is Cummings suggesting that calling the dead 'heroes' can rectify the injustice? Perhaps he's reflecting that the patriotic soldiers were 'happy' before their deaths, since they had not questioned their involvement in the conflict.

Imagery

'Who rushed like lions to the roaring slaughter' combines alliterative letters 'r' and 'l' with a **simile**. 'The dead' have run towards battle as lions charging for a kill.

America is **personified** in line 7 and again in line 13 with 'the voice of liberty'. If freedom has a voice, the poet pleads, then why isn't it speaking out, to stop the politicians making decisions that cause so much bloodshed for all countries concerned?

Ideas to consider

In 1926 when this poem was published, anti-war sentiments would be considered unpatriotic and shocking. Nowadays public protest about a government's decision to go to war is more common.

Can you suggest why 'thy' (l. 7) changes to the modern version 'your'?

Do you think that lack of punctuation makes you concentrate more on alternative interpretations of the poem?

'The charge of the Light Brigade' by Alfred Lord Tennyson

Context

Tennyson was born in Lincolnshire in 1809 and died in 1892. He was Poet Laureate of the United Kingdom in 1884, when he read a newspaper report of a heroic defeat in 1854 and in response wrote 'The charge of the Light Brigade', a dramatic tribute to the 673 British cavalrymen at the Battle of Balaclava in the Crimean War. Owing to a military blunder, they rode courageously into 'the valley of death' against Russian artillery on all sides, knowing they were doomed from the start.

The Crimean was the first media war, where journalists reported events in a way that had never previously happened. An eyewitness reporter for *The Times* wrote 'Surely that handful of men were not going to charge an army in position? Alas, it was but too true — their desperate valour knew no bounds'.

Glossary

half a league (l. 1)
about one and a half miles

dismay'd (l. 10)
lacking courage

sabres (l. 27)
curved swords, used by cavalry

battery-smoke (l. 33)
smoke from the lines of guns

Cossack (l. 34)
Russian cavalryman

What happens?

From the very beginning of the poem the reader is thrown into the action. The 600 cavalry are ordered to 'Charge for the guns!' by an unnamed 'he' (the identity of whoever gave the mistaken order for the charge was never proved, but the command to 'take the guns' was meant to order an attack on one valley flank to retrieve captured ally guns). The common soldiers know that they are being asked to sacrifice themselves by charging into blazing gunfire, but they follow rules without question because of their sense of loyalty and duty. They ride well, but their swords are useless against Russian gunfire from both sides of the valley and rows of cannons facing them. Nevertheless, they charge through these, before turning to ride back, still 'Storm'd at with shot and shell'. The survivors return, sadly reduced in number, but the poet praises their bravery and commands that the Light Brigade be honoured.

Relief of the Light Brigade by Richard Caton Woodville

Structure

The six stanzas vary from six to eleven lines, the longest being the fourth, which describes the valiant attempt of the outnumbered cavalry to charge a line of guns and a waiting enemy army. The shortest and final stanza addresses the reader, to 'wonder' at such patriotic obedience. Perhaps its shortness echoes the brevity of the young 'noble' lives lost.

Tennyson uses a **dactylic metre** (/0 0, one stressed followed by two unstressed syllables) to give the effect of a cavalry charge.

Forward, the**/Light** Bri gade
Was there a**/man** dis may'd?

To understand the effectiveness of the metre you need to read the poem aloud. This is a well-known poem, probably because of its galloping rhythm.

When the lines end with the insistent, but not always perfect, rhymes however: 'onward', 'hundred', 'blunder'd', 'thundered', 'wondered', the second foot changes to two (trochaic) beats (/0) to stress the word at the end and clip the line — '**All** the world/**won** der'd'. Note how the letter 'e' is omitted to make sure that readers don't stress the syllable 'ed' in its archaic way.

Stanzas three and five are very similarly structured with repeated lines to begin, but 'Cannon in front of them' (l. 0) has to change alarmingly to 'Canon behind them' (l. 1) to emphasise the need to retreat while still under fire. The alteration at the end of the stanzas tells the sad story. 'Rode the six hundred' (l. 6) becomes:

All that was left of them,
Left of six hundred (ll. 48, 49)

Language and imagery

Along with the rhythm, the poem relies on **repetition** for the dramatic effect of military precision. 'Theirs not to…' in lines 13, 14 and 15, makes it clear that to question the ludicrous command from an officer, although 'someone had blunder'd' would not have been considered, when Victorian military values meant service at all costs. The repetition of 'Cannon to…' describes the full horror of the situation. 'All the world wonder'd' (ll. 1, 52) is repeated to stress disbelief not only of the soldiers, but also of the world when reports of the disaster reach home.

Alliteration gives the effect of whistling bullets in 'Storm'd at with shot and shell' and **metaphors** describe the terror of the charge. The 'valley of Death' (l. 7) echoes the words of Psalm 23, inferring little hope of survival, and extends into 'the jaws of Death' (l. 24) and 'the mouth of Hell' (l. 25) suggesting further that the unfortunate cavalry are being offered up as sacrifices.

The last line in each stanza narrates the progress of events. 'Rode the six hundred' (ll. 8, 17, 26) changes to 'Not the six hundred' (l. 38) as the fighting takes its toll, resulting in 'Left of six hundred' on their depleted return. The exclamation 'Noble six hundred!' insists that the cavalry be raised to heroic status.

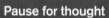

Ideas to consider

As Poet Laureate, Tennyson had to remain patriotic and in favour with the Crown, yet with lines 12 and 52 he allows the reader to question the waste of life in this atrocity caused by blundering officers. Do you think the ambiguity of the line is effective?

The numbers slaughtered in the First and Second World Wars completely overshadow this minor battle, where fewer than two hundred died. It was the idea of a chivalric charge of cavalry and officers in full-dress uniforms trying to compete with modern fire arms that caught the public's — and Tennyson's — imagination, at the time.

'The falling leaves' by Margaret Postgate Cole

Context

Dame Margaret Cole was born in Cambridge in 1893 and died in 1980. She wrote about politics and history and became a pacifist. She campaigned against military conscription when her brother (whose claims to be recognised as a conscientious objector had been rejected) was jailed for refusing military orders. In the 1930s she gave up her pacifist views, however, in response to the Third Reich in Germany and Franco's dictatorship in Spain. 'The falling leaves' was written in autumn 1915.

What happens?

The poet observes the dead leaves dropping from the trees on a still autumn afternoon and it sadly brings to mind the many soldiers who have also fallen in First World War battles.

Structure

The 12 lines, although punctuated by commas and a semi-colon, are all one sentence, probably to suggest the poet's preoccupation with the one idea. There is a strict rhyme scheme, which divides the poem into two: ABC, ABC, then DEF, DEF. The first six lines describe the falling leaves and the second six compare them to the 'multitude' of 'slain' soldiers. The tight rhyme pattern gives the sombre mood of an elegy or lament for the dead.

Throughout, the strong iambic metre adds to this sad, thoughtful mood: odd lines each have three iambic feet (0/0/0/), whereas even lines are in iambic pentameter (0/0/0/0/0/).

Glossary

thence (l. 7)
from that place

slain (l. 10)
killed

pestilence (l. 10)
disease

strewed (l. 11)
spread

Flemish clay (l. 12)
Belgian earth (where many First World War battles were fought)

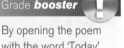

Grade **booster**

By opening the poem with the word 'Today' we are immediately aware that the poet has a story to tell us. The use of the pronoun 'I', which follows, turns the poem into an autobiographical narrative.

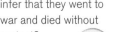

Language and imagery

To the poet the leaves **symbolise** the huge numbers of brave soldiers, all losing their lives and their beauty as they rot on the battlefields. The 'brown leaves' (l. 2) suggest khaki uniforms and 'whistling' (l. 4) has echoes of the soldiers whistling as they marched away to war. 'Noon' is probably chosen since it's the time of day when the sun is at its highest point in the sky, just as the soldiers are in the prime of youth.

Soft letter sounds keep the poem gently thoughtful. 'No **w**ind **wh**irled them **wh**istling to the sky' (l. 4) relies on **alliteration** and the **onomatopoeic** sound of the breathy 'wh', while the final line uses a sustained 'f' to emphasise the soundless fall of snowflakes, which will melt away as quickly as young lives are lost.

Two **similes** compare the falling leaves to 'snowflakes wiping out the noon' and dead soldiers to 'snowflakes falling on the Flemish clay'. When snow falls, it quickly and 'thickly' covers the earth in the way that a 'multitude' of bodies in fierce battle soon lie 'slain' on the cold earth. Just like the beautiful snowflakes, their innocent lives would disappear.

Cole in this poem obviously considers war to be futile. There is no reason, she argues, why young men had to die — 'no wind of age or pestilence'. The word 'gallant', however, shows her respect for those who had to fight.

> ### Pause for thought
>
> Do you think the use of 'silently' (l. 5) could also infer that they went to war and died without protest?

Relationships

Contemporary poems

'Brothers' by Andrew Forster

Context

Andrew Forster was born in 1964 and grew up in Rotherham in South Yorkshire, but has lived in Scotland since 1987. 'Brothers' is in his first collection of poetry, entitled *Fear of Thunder*, published in 2007.

Asked why he wrote the poem, Forster said:

> 'Brothers' was one of a number of poems based on childhood memories that I wrote in a group. I'd never really written about childhood and suddenly I was faced with these extraordinarily vivid memories. The more I wrote the more the memories just kept on coming.
>
> I'm sure that all of us who have brothers and sisters have occasionally behaved in ways we've later regretted. As a poet I'm interested in exploring tiny moments that seem to have huge significance. The incident in 'Brothers' seemed to be one of those moments.

> ### Glossary
>
> **Saddled (l. 1)**
> burdened
>
> **ambled (l. 2)**
> to walk at a slow easy pace
>
> **threadbare (l. 2)**
> overused to the point of being worn out
>
> **tank-top (l. 4)**
> a sleeveless knitted jumper, worn over a shirt

What happens?

The nine-year-old narrator and his ten-year-old friend have been given the responsibility of looking after the narrator's six-year-old brother for the afternoon. As they head towards the bus stop the little brother realises he hasn't any bus fare and is told to go home and get some. The two older boys, feeling very grown-up as they watch the six-year-old running back home, dash to catch the approaching bus, knowingly leaving the young brother behind. The narrator still remembers how he 'ran on' and reflects that his failure to show brotherly concern and kindness towards his brother on this memorable occasion may have been the start of their future differences.

Structure

The poem is written in three stanzas of **free verse** with one example of **end rhyme** on lines 2 and 4. These, combined with the final 'p' of 'cup' on line 3, introduce the story. After this, events begin to unwind, the poet's sense of unease develops and there is no further end rhyme.

Line 9 contains **internal rhyme**, however:

His smile, like mine, said I was nine and he was ten

Here the close positioning of the rhymes 'mine' and 'nine' give out a mood of smugness at the moment the boys have 'got rid' of their charge.

Language and imagery

The poem is written in the past tense, since the incident is a recount of an event that happened in the poet's childhood. It is probably autobiographical, so we shall assume that the narrator is Forster.

Forster remembers how disgruntled he was that he had to look after his younger brother. Words such as 'saddled' (l. 1), 'ridiculous' (l. 4) and 'spouting' (l. 5) **contrast** with the language used to describe the two older friends. They 'ambled' talking about football; they knew they had to 'stroll the town' to look cool 'as grown-ups do'. The six year-old, in their opinion, didn't know what he was talking about and still wore unfashionable clothes. Only a young child, who had to wear what somebody had knitted for him, would go out wearing such an embarrassing 'tank-top'.

It is also interesting to note the difference between the **verbs** used to describe the actions of the boys. The older two made sure they moved casually in a self-conscious way. It was important that they were seen to be 'cool'. The younger brother, on the other hand, was delighted to be out for the afternoon with the older boys and 'skipped' and 'windmilled'.

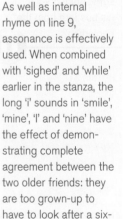

Grade **booster**

As well as internal rhyme on line 9, assonance is effectively used. When combined with 'sighed' and 'while' earlier in the stanza, the long 'i' sounds in 'smile', 'mine', 'I' and 'nine' have the effect of demonstrating complete agreement between the two older friends: they are too grown-up to have to look after a six-year-old for the day.

A strong **visual image** is created by the **metaphor** 'windmilled', as the little boy charges back home, his hands wildly rotating. In his innocence he does not suspect that the other boys were annoyed to have him with them and are likely to leave him behind. Other visual descriptions give clear pictures to the reader. 'The threadbare field' can be imagined as the local space used as a play area and football pitch. The word 'froze' on line 6, gives an instant picture of the little boy's realisation that he has not got any money to catch the bus with the others. The word 'crested' describes the sudden appearance of the bus as it gets to the top of the hill. Most poignant is probably the picture of the little boy on lines 12 and 13.

Looking back I saw you spring towards the gate,
your hand holding out what must have been a coin.

The little lad has got his bus fare and is excited about his trip into town with the older boys. We can imagine his despair and disbelief as he realises they are going to go without him. His moving gesture of holding out the coin as proof that he can come too is probably the image that keeps returning to the poet and is responsible for the guilt he now feels. As an adult he is able to recognise how unkind and unfair his actions were on this particular day.

The **metaphor** on the final line relies on the word 'distance', which implies not only the physical space between the boys running for the bus and the six-year-old still on his garden path, but also the developing differences in the relationship between Forster and his brother.

Proper nouns, such as 'Sheffield Wednesday' and 'Rotherham United' place the memory firmly in time and place, just as when somebody recounts a personal story. 'We chased Olympic Gold' describes the imaginative pursuits of the two friends, giving their athletic best to reach the bus stop before the bus arrives. They are still children and, although they want to seem like 'grown-ups', they do not yet have the maturity to recognise their responsibility and wait for the little boy.

Ideas to consider

Why does Forster treat his brother so unkindly? He most probably loved his brother, yet was prepared to hurt him. The next poem in the collection of poetry is called 'At the circus with my brother'. When their mother presents the two brothers with tickets to go to the circus, Forster writes, 'I forgot you were only my younger brother'. He goes on to say they were 'equals for the evening'. When he wants to go somewhere special and taking a friend is not an option, then his younger brother is no longer an encumbrance. Do we all have separate rules and behave differently when we are with our friends?

Pause for thought

Do you think the older boys meant to be so cruel? Did the idea of leaving the younger boy behind occur only when the bus arrived and he hadn't returned? Perhaps they had sufficient money for his bus fare from the beginning?

PHILIP ALLAN LITERATURE GUIDE **FOR GCSE**

'Ghazal' by Mimi Khalvati

Context

Mimi Khalvati was born in Tehran, Iran, in 1944, but moved to school on the Isle of Wight when she was six. She started writing poetry in her forties and has also worked as an actor and director in the UK and Iran.

A ghazal (rhyming with muzzle) is a poem that can be sung. It always deals with the one theme: love — and usually unattainable love. This form of poetry is very old and goes as far back as seventh-century Arabia. Since the 1990s poets have begun to experiment with the ghazal form in the English language.

Glossary

woo (l. 2) be romantic towards somebody

refrain (l. 3) a repeated section at the end of each verse/stanza

venomous (l. 7) spiteful

laurel (l. 9) a plant worn on the head to symbolise victory/achievement

marry (l. 13) match

Shamsuddin and Rumi (l. 18) were very close friends in thirteenth-century Persia. Rumi expressed his love for Shamsuddin, and grief at his death, through music, dance and poems, many of which were ghazals.

What happens?

The poem is an expression of love, inviting 'my love' to take possession of the speaker's heart and mind.

The feelings of love in a traditional ghazal do not usually express physical desire, being only spiritual, but some of these lines could be understood to be suggesting (very subtly, yet sensuously) a desired physical relationship. Whether you interpret the poem this way or not is not important: it is essential, however, that you back up your ideas with relevant quotation and explanation.

Structure

'Ghazal' begins with a rhyming couplet, in which the last two syllables of line 2, 'woo me', rhyme with the second line of each of the other two-line stanzas: 'cue me', 'tattoo me', 'subdue me' etc.

This poem follows other ghazal rules: there should be no enjambement between stanzas, each stanza being completely self-contained; and the poet's name ('Mimi' or 'twice the me' in this ghazal) should be skilfully incorporated into the final stanza.

Pause for thought

Each long line contains 12 syllables and the stanzas are all in pairs. When the poem is read aloud, therefore, it has to be read slowly for the longing mood to be heard and felt. Try reading it quickly — can you make it sound romantic?

Language and imagery

Although no enjambement can be used between stanzas in the ghazal form, it is sometimes used effectively within a couplet. Examine the following example:

> If you are the rhyme and I the refrain, don't hang
> on my lips, come and I'll come too when you cue me (ll. 3, 4)

The natural pause at the end of the line gives the impression of dropping down to the next line and the words 'on my lips' come as a complete surprise. The strong wait at the end of line 13, on the other hand, allows the metaphors 'hawk to my shadow, moth to my flame' to be introduced, before the question 'What shape should I take to marry your own, have you' is completed with 'pursue me?'. The clever way of introducing the poet's name 'Mimi' also relies on the pause after 'twice the me' before 'I am', to complete the wordplay.

Each couplet is like a short poem on its own and contains its own **metaphor(s)** to express the poet's longing.

> If I am the laurel leaf in your crown, you are
> the arms around my bark, arms that never knew me.

Here the poet is alluding to Apollo, the Greek god of music and poetry, who fell in love with the nymph Daphne and chased her through the forest. Nature changed Daphne into a laurel tree, which Apollo embraced, taking its branches for a crown and announcing that, just as the evergreen leaves would never die, so his love would last for ever.

The speaker here imagines herself as the laurel tree wrapped in her hero's arms, although she admits that, like Apollo and Daphne, they have never yet shared a physical embrace.

Apollo and Daphne by Gian Lorenzo Bernini, 1625

- 'When the arrow flies, the heart is pierced, tattoo me' (l. 6) gives a visual image of a heart-shaped tattoo with diagonal arrows through it — not a single sharp attack but the result of many piercings.
- Lines 13 and 14 contain romantic images of the close shadow preceding the hawk in flight, or the moth attracted to a flame and dancing in its brightness.
- The love-smitten persona imagines the delights of being refreshed by dew dropped in the shade of the old, but still leafy, tree.

The second line in the couplet regularly surprises, often using **imperative verbs** to entice the listener into the relationship — 'subdue', 'bedew', 'pursue', 'renew' — all rhyming words to fulfil the rules of the ghazal form.

Ideas to consider

Khalvati likes to read her poems aloud so that the musical sounds of the words can be enjoyed. She says that at times her poems are 'soothing, soporific even'. Do you agree?

In a traditional ghazal the speaker is aware that his/her love is unattainable, yet still continues loving. There are hints in this poem that love is not going to be returned. How could you interpret the last stanza?

'Harmonium' by Simon Armitage

Context

Armitage often uses his own background and experiences for his poems and here he remembers an incident with his father. He used to sing to the harmonium when he was a choirboy in Marsden church.

Glossary

Harmonium (title) a small organ with a keyboard, on which sound is produced by bellows forcing air over reeds, worked by pedals

Farrand Chapelette (l. 1) a make of organ manufactured in USA in 1887

'for a song' (l. 4) for very little money

beatify (l. 6) to make into a saint, to make blessed

treadles (l. 10) pedals operated by the feet

harmonics (l. 13) pleasing musical sound

gilded (l. 17) golden

finches (l. 17) small colourful songbirds

nave (l. 23) the central part of a church

freight (l. 24) a burden, a load

What happens?

An old church organ is waiting to be disposed of and the narrator decides to buy it. The organ has aged over the hundred years that it has accompanied the voices of generations of families in the church choir, but it can still be played. The poet's father (presumably Armitage's father) comes to help carry the organ away and, as the organ is carried 'on its back', the older man comments that the next time his son will carry a wooden box through the church will be at his father's funeral. The son is unable to make any meaningful reply.

Structure

The poem consists of four stanzas of varied length, the final stanza, which deals with the relationship between father and son, being the longest. The **metre** is a combination of anapaest (00-) and iambic feet (0-), which are ideal for telling a story, since they have a strong rhythm without the comical effect often produced by pure anapaest metre. At times the stress changes to emphasise a word:

> **Sun** light,/through stained **glass,**/which **day**/to **day**
> could be **a**/ti fy **saints**/and **raise**/the **dead** (ll. 5, 6)

For the description at the start of the second stanza, the metre of the first bar changes, throwing the emphasis onto '**Sun**light' as though beginning a story.

Another effective change of rhythm is in the middle of line 21 — 'And we carry it flat, laid on its back' — where the pause before 'laid' gives a feeling of physical exertion as the organ is turned over.

The combination of heavy rhythm, **single syllables** and **internal rhyme** on line 24, 'will bear the **freight** of his own dead **weight**', also sounds cumbersome, and we can imagine the doleful voice of the father and two men clumsily carrying the wooden organ through the church. 'Throats', at the end of line 16, rhymes with 'notes' in the middle of line 17, leaving a poignant pause before 'had streamed out', to describe the ease with which the choristers sang. Most of the poem, otherwise, is in **free verse**, but the two final lines **rhyme** to give a sense of finality to the poem, suggesting nothing more was ever said and, perhaps, to express regret that communication between father and son was usually short and inadequate.

Language and imagery

A **theme of ageing** runs through the poem, leading to death in the final stanza. The instrument that had provided such joy and harmony over the years 'was gathering dust' and 'was due to be bundled off'. The case of the harmonium is 'aged', the keys 'yellowed' and 'holes were worn' in the pedals. Similarly, the father has 'dottled thumbs' and is anticipating his own 'dead weight', when he too will be 'starved of breath'. 'Dottled' usually means 'confused as a result of age' in **dialect** speech — similar to 'dotty', so probably suggests a certain amount of fumbling as the older man tries to lift and carry the harmonium.

The harmonium is **personified** in lines 8 and 9. The 'fingernails' or 'ends' of the keys are now yellow and one of the notes no longer plays, having 'lost its tongue'. But there are memories still in the ambiguity of 'still struck a chord' of a time when generations of the same families had sung their choral music so melodiously. The **simile** 'gilded finches — like high notes — had streamed out' makes the singing sound angelic and reminds the reader of lines 5 and 6 where the sunlight on the stained-glass windows lit up the haloes of the saints.

The beauty of the past seems to contrast with the sad reality of the present in the mind of the poet. On line 18 he observes that the father does not open his throat to sing, but arrives in 'his own blue cloud of tobacco smog, /with smoker's fingers'.

Ideas to consider

The two men know each other well and this is explained implicitly:

> And he, being him… (l. 2)

> And I, being me… (l. 5)

The reference to death, probably made frequently now by the father, is an uncomfortable subject for the son. He knows there is little that can be said to offer true comfort — just 'some shallow or sorry phrase or word', so he dismisses the remark, while struggling under the weight of the harmonium. He is literally 'starved of breath' with his exertions, and the father, obviously a heavy smoker, will find breathing difficult. The last three lines suggest something more, however. The son probably knows he should have talked to his father, that there were real fears that needed addressing, yet, as always, he chose to make light of the situation.

'Hour' by Carol Ann Duffy

Context

Carol Ann Duffy was born in 1955 in Glasgow and read philosophy at Liverpool University. A poet, playwright, reviewer and broadcaster, she presently lives and works in Manchester. She is considered one of Britain's most successful and popular poets and became Poet Laureate in 2009. 'Hour' and 'Quickdraw' are both in her anthology named *Rapture*, winner

Midas (l. 6)

In Greek mythology, everything that King Midas touched turned to gold

back handing (l. 8)

paying someone money illegally in order to encourage them to do something

cuckoo spit (l. 10)

blobs of white frothy liquid on stems and leaves

of the 2005 T. S. Eliot prize. Throughout *Rapture* the poems tell a love story, from the first stages of the romance to the end of the relationship.

What happens?

This is a very romantic and intimate poem, describing two lovers who have just an hour to spend together one summer's day. They lie in a 'grass ditch' kissing passionately and, although they know they do not have long together, their love seems to hold back the passage of time.

Structure

Duffy uses a traditional English (or Elizabethan or Shakespearean) sonnet format for her love poem. This consists of 14 lines, divided into three quatrains (four-lined stanzas) and an end couplet. The rhyme scheme also fits the tight sonnet pattern: abab cdcd efef gg, the second and fourth lines of each stanza having a perfect rhyme, while the first and third rely on half rhymes. The final two lines rhyme — 'poor' and 'straw' — and cleverly sum up the previous 12 lines. (Note: in some parts of the UK, 'poor' is pronounced to rhyme with 'straw'.)

The metre is irregular, a combination of iambic and anapaestic metres. Lines 6 and 9 alone conform to the iambic pentameter pattern. These two lines:

> like treasure on the ground like Midas light (l. 6)

> So nothing dark will end our shining hour (l. 9)

in their regularity bring a particularly romantic mood to the experience.

Language and imagery

Grade **booster**

'Love's not Time's fool' Shakespeare writes in his Sonnet 116. Duffy starts 'Hour' with 'Love's time's beggar'. She places the stress on the first word as though responding to Shakespeare's sonnet, written over 400 years earlier.

The first eight lines employ an **extended metaphor** where time is personified as a rich person handing out precious units of time to people in love. It is a passionate poem implying that all time spent apart from the one you love is poor in comparison to time spent together.

In the first four lines Duffy **personifies** love as a beggar always asking for more time to enjoy being with the one you love. With the **simile** 'bright as a dropped coin' she compares 'a single hour' to a coin that, dropped on the ground in front of a beggar, 'makes love rich'. The word 'spend' can be understood to mean the literal spending of money or as a **metaphor** for choosing quality time — 'the whole of the summer sky and a grass ditch'. The idea of a ditch at the end of the lengthy fourth line is unexpected, but it makes the affair more realistic and down-to-earth, in contrast to the romantic presents of flowers and wine.

Stanza two begins by juxtaposing (placing side by side) 'thousands of seconds', again an unusual way of suggesting that they stretch the time they have and make each second count. 'Millionaires back handing the night' (l. 8) continues the **money theme**, suggesting that lovers slip extra payments to night (a personified time-lender) to bribe him to wait so that 'Time slows'. The poet or the persona of the poem has the ability, like King Midas, to turn her lover's hair, arms and legs golden: 'your hair/like treasure on the ground like Midas light/turning your limbs to gold.' These **similes** are sensual in their description and traditional in sonnet content, where poets would exaggerate their lovers' physical characteristics for romantic purposes.

Stanza three continues the theme of Midas light in 'our shining hour'. Love lights up the scene and the earthy image of 'cuckoo spit/hung from a blade of grass at your ear' is brighter than any jewel, chandelier or spotlight. The image of blobs of froth, unromantically called cuckoo spit, remind the reader that these two lovers are not in a traditional romantic setting, but lying, away from the eyes of the world, in their one precious hour of time — in a grassy ditch.

It is the image of grass again, combined with the money theme, that ends the final couplet, in the form of straw: 'love spins gold, gold, gold from straw' uses the trio of words for dramatic effect. The **repetition** of 'gold', whether echoing the theme of wealth or beauty or light, suggests that love creates the very best that life has to offer. 'Now.' on line 13, is set alone, probably to restrict the love to the very moment in time that is being described — 'a single hour' in which time has no power over love.

> **Pause for thought**
>
> 'Time hates love, wants love poor' (l. 13) — simple single-syllable words have a complex meaning. Can you explain what the poet is saying and how she turns the idea around in the last line?

Ideas to consider

A children's fairy story, 'Rumpelstiltskin', tells the tale of a miller's daughter who is shut in a tower room and commanded by the king to spin straw into gold, since her boastful father had lied that she could. A dwarf appears nightly and spins the straw into gold. Perhaps Duffy is suggesting that love is as magical as a fairy story, turning everyday experiences into times to treasure.

The poems in the anthology *Rapture* tell the story of a love affair from beginning to end and are very personal in the way they describe the poet's/persona's feelings. Do you think 'our shining hour' (l. 9) can relate to other people's experience of love?

'In Paris with you' by James Fenton

Context

Born in Lincoln in 1949 and educated at Magdalen College, Oxford, James Fenton was the Oxford Professor of Poetry from 1994 until 1999. As

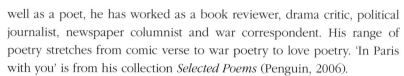

well as a poet, he has worked as a book reviewer, drama critic, political journalist, newspaper columnist and war correspondent. His range of poetry stretches from comic verse to war poetry to love poetry. 'In Paris with you' is from his collection *Selected Poems* (Penguin, 2006).

Paul Theroux, an American travel writer, says Fenton's poems are 'passionate and personal...always full of the pleasures of the language'.

What happens?

The speaker is disillusioned with love at the beginning of the poem. He (we may presume the speaker is male, but could easily be female) feels cheated by a previous relationship and admits he has come to Paris 'on the rebound'. He is 'a hostage' who has no interest in the tourist sites most visitors want to see, preferring to stay in the shabby hotel to get to know his new girlfriend (again we presume he is speaking to a woman, although the gender is not specified). 'Let's talk of Paris' he says in stanza five, although he has shown no interest in Paris previously and the only view he has is that of a cheap 'sleazy' hotel room. In stanza six, Paris symbolises the 'love' that, earlier that same day, he did not want to talk about. Now he is captivated by the woman and starts to make love to her. Paris has suddenly become the most romantic place on earth.

Structure

The first two stanzas have a jaunty heavy rhythm and lines 2 and 5 rhyme, as do lines 3 and 4. The whole effect suggests song lyrics, needing to be sung not read. Stanza three appears to be conforming to the same pattern, but cuts quickly to stanza four, which is different, almost like a chorus in the middle of a song. Perhaps this is the point where he takes more of an interest in his travelling companion, so the form changes. But only temporarily. Stanza five picks up the enthusiasm to 'talk of Paris' and the rhythm and rhyming pattern of the opening stanzas returns. The final stanza throws in an extra line, (line 29), as an aside. 'Am I embarrassing you?' he asks, in the middle of his passionate advances, and the reader also has to pause, before the final statement.

Language and imagery

Fenton uses **colloquial** expressions in the first half of the poem. He has 'had an earful' and has 'downed a drink or two'. He is in no mood for travelling and certainly shows no interest in the attractions of the romantic city of Paris. In fact, he is making little effort to be polite to his companion. The use of 'marooned' instead of 'marooned' in order to rhyme the line with 'wounded' gives instant comic effect, which continues with the use of 'bamboozled' on line 6. The reader has little sympathy with the speaker, who enjoys indulging in his own misfortune and whose previous affair seems to lack seriousness. 'Do you mind..../If we say sod off to sodding Notre Dame' emphasises his dejected mood. 'Notre Dame' is a huge towering place of worship on an island in the middle of the Seine. Parisians love their cathedral and people travel from all over the world to attend its masses and enjoy its beautiful interior. The idea of not wanting to explore the cathedral or even to walk down the wide Champs Elysées, to sit at a pavement cafe and watch the world go by, seems surprising — but to use the slang words 'sod off' and 'sodding' is shocking and highlights the speaker's sulky mood. Once inside the hotel room, he overlooks the rundown fabric of the building and recognises the desirability of his companion. He no longer uses informal language: he is so polite in his attentions that he even asks whether he is 'embarrassing' her with his endearments.

The romantic Champs Elysées in Paris

Fenton often uses **repetition** in the same way that song lyrics rely on key lines being repeated.

- 'Don't talk to me of love' at the start of the last two stanzas has a different connotation to the earlier protestations in stanza one and introduces the irony of the situation. He means exactly the opposite of what he says. Paris suddenly represents romance and he now wants all the attractions that Paris can offer, as long as it is 'the little bit of Paris in "his" view'. He has forgotten he is 'one of your talking wounded' and is embarking on his next love affair.

Learning who you are,
Learning what I am.

suggests he has an interest in getting to know all about his new girlfriend, but the last two stanzas with the repetition of 'I'm in Paris' and his listing of physical attributes, demonstrates that he has little interest in talking about anything as the poem ends humorously. He has obviously forgotten his previous love already and is moving enthusiastically on to his next.

Ideas to consider

Cole Porter (1881–1964) was a very popular American songwriter who lived in Paris when he was a young man. His songs have snappy tunes, clever rhymes and witty, humorous lyrics. Do you think Fenton, who also writes song lyrics and operettas, is playing with words and ideas in a similar way? You can read the words of 'I love Paris' and 'Let's not talk

> **Pause for thought**
>
> Could the poet be asking whether he is also embarrassing the reader when he refers to 'all points south'?

about love' by searching for them on the internet. You can also hear Frank Sinatra and Doris Day singing 'I love Paris' with romantic pictures of Paris on YouTube:

www.youtube.com/watch?v=WF_yN1R2b5M

Listen to the clever lyrics of 'Let's not talk about love' here:

www.youtube.com/watch?v=4Ocp4yO6BjY

Some people might think that a hotel room with a crack across the ceiling and wallpaper peeling from the walls is not a very romantic setting, but the clue is in the word 'sleazy', which suggests the hotel is a little disreputable. It is this lack of respectability in a European city that makes an affair more exciting.

'Praise song for my mother' by Grace Nichols

Context

Grace Nichols was born in a small coastal village in Guyana in 1950. When she was eight years old she moved with her family to Georgetown, the capital of Guyana, where she experienced her country's fight for independence from the UK, eventually gained in 1966. She worked as a teacher and journalist, which nurtured an interest in the folk stories and traditions of Guyana. When she was 27, she emigrated with her partner, the poet John Agard, and her daughter to the UK, where she still lives.

Nichols enjoys exploring cultural differences in the subjects and language of her poems, writing in standard English and Guyanese Creole (the language resulting from a mixture of other languages). Her ancestors were African slaves and praise songs are a traditional form of African poem that can be accompanied by music (often drums) and chanted or sung.

Glossary

fathoming (l. 3) encircling with the arms/ embracing; understanding the meaning of/ getting to the bottom of something difficult to understand; working out the depth of deep water

grained (l. 6) having a lined, textured surface

mantling (l. 6) enveloping; wrapping in a cloak

flame tree (l. 12) tree with bright red or yellow flowers

plantain (l. 13) a banana-like fruit that is cooked before being eaten

replenishing (l. 14) filling up again; making complete again

What happens?

The poet praises her mother in a number of separate images, all linked to her secure, happy and colourful childhood and adolescence in Guyana. She finishes the song in admiration of her mother's aspirations for her children when she tells them to go to their 'wide futures'.

Structure

This praise song is composed of free verse stanzas describing the poet's mother. The first three stanzas have the same three-lined shape, beginning with 'You were' and introducing a metaphor on the second line that is further described using adjectives on line three. The fourth stanza, however, is longer, with three lines of metaphors and the repeated (participial) adjective 'replenishing replenishing' stretches out to the right, probably suggesting that the mother's generous nurturing was never-ending and went far beyond what could ever be expected. The last line is set apart to emphasise the shift from the description of the mother's praise-worthy characteristics to a spoken line. Having provided a very loving and secure childhood, she now wants her children to be independent of her — 'Go to your wide futures, you said'. To allow and expect a young person to make his or her own way in life without parental interference is perhaps one of the hardest, but most valuable, things a parent can give.

Rhythm is important in a praise song, but rhyme is not. Read this poem out aloud and hear the regular repetitive metre of the first three stanzas and then the way the metre speeds up in stanza four as the list of qualities builds, giving the feeling that the mother never stopped loving and giving — until the last line, which is effective since it is unexpected.

Language and imagery

Each stanza gives one or more 'praise names', in the form of vivid **metaphors** of some aspect of the person. Ancient and medieval teachings believed the universe and human body were made up of four elements: water, air, fire and earth. Nichols describes her mother as being the source of all these essential elements — all necessary for life.

> You were/water to me

The adjectives 'deep', 'bold', 'fathoming' rely on many connotations for their full effect. As well as their literal meanings, they also suggest depth of emotions, a courageous attitude to life and a sense of the ability to understand the feelings of a growing child.

> You were/moon's eye to me

The earth and the moon exert equal gravitational forces on each other, in the same way that a mother and child have a special bond. The moon orbits the earth in the way a concerned parent watches attentively over her child. 'Grained' might suggest the cratered appearance of the moon from the earth as well as the texture of mature skin, and 'mantling' conjures up ideas of protection and security, a comforting light through night's darkness.

Pause for thought

A 14-lined poem with a concise form, a sonnet, is an ideal form for a love poem. This poem has 15 lines, with line 14 almost breaking free of the shape. Could it be regarded as a sonnet?

You were/sunrise to me

Each morning, the sun can be relied upon to rise and bring the warmth of the day. The sun is also symbolic of life and energy, while 'streaming' praises the constant supply of affection in the way the Guyanese sun would pour down its rays.

You were/the fishes red gill to me

A fish breathes water in through its gills in order to absorb oxygen, in a similar way to how an unborn baby survives in the womb. Is Nichols saying that her mother gave her the most essential thing in life: air to breathe? This stanza is also full of the senses: sight, touch, taste and smell — the vibrant colours of the fish and flame tree; the cool shade of the tree's branches; the flavour of the crab's leg; and the delicious smell of the 'fried plantain' (an important part of the Guyanese diet).

The repetition of 'replenishing' sums up all the mother's qualities previously celebrated and stresses the idea that so much was constantly and freely given. The adult daughter knows her mother not only fed her good food, but nourished her with knowledge, wisdom, strength, confidence and many other qualities that are essential for maturity.

Alliteration is used effectively at times. 'Moon's eye…mantling' has the repeated 'm' sound, which has a warm, comforting sound; the sustained sibilant 's' in 'sunrise… streaming' has a flowing sound; while another sustained letter — 'f' in 'fishes…flame…fried' — introduces the idea of fullness before the repeated use of 'replenishing'.

Ideas to consider

In our Western culture we do not have an equivalent form of poetry to the praise song, but we do have a eulogy, which is usually written in prose and read or delivered by a relative or close friend to praise and honour somebody who has died, perhaps as part of a funeral service. Do you think the 'praise song' form of poetry is effective for such a tribute?

Nichols says: 'I am a writer across two worlds; I just can't forget my Caribbean culture and past, so there's this constant interaction between the two worlds.' How much of 'Praise song for my mother' do you think could describe a British mother?

'Quickdraw' by Carol Ann Duffy

Context

'Quickdraw' is another poem from Duffy's collection of poetry called *Rapture*, (see p. 51) which charts a love affair from its beginning to its end. 'Hour' describes feelings at the beginning of the affair, whereas

'Quickdraw' is obviously at a later, problematic, stage in the relationship.

What happens?

'Quickdraw' tells the story of a fierce argument between two lovers. Narrated in the first person, the battle is played out like a Western shoot-out, where phones replace guns. Harsh words by text inflict increasing pain and, only at the end, at the point where the narrator is distraught with misery, convinced that there is no hope left for the relationship, is reconciliation made. Harsh words are finally replaced by text messages of many kisses — a passionate ceasefire by phone.

Structure

The poem is written in sixteen lines of free verse, in four stanzas. The first three stanzas have an irregular shape, since each has a short line. It may be coincidental that they appear gun shaped, but the effect of placing 'you've wounded me' on a separate line after the 'groan' is not. Another enforced break after 'then blast me' ensures the reader has to pause before the dramatic phrase 'through the heart'. The erratic pace has the feel of a gun fight, where the action speeds and slows. The shape of the last stanza returns to normality as the caller stops fighting and tries to heal the wounds with kisses.

Occasional **enjambement** and frequent **punctuation** aid the varying pace: 'You ring, quickdraw, your voice a pellet/in my ear' (ll. 3, 4). Here the commas insist on pauses to give the effect of the phone being hastily grabbed from a hip pocket. The short sentences 'You text them both at once. I reel' (l. 13) produces a staccato effect to illustrate total panic as the phones shrill together.

Duffy skilfully integrates rhyme, half-rhyme and internal rhyme into the poem. The first six lines contain the words 'phones', 'alone', 'groan', 'tone', 'phone', creating a storytelling feeling, while only 'groan' and 'phone' are line end rhymes. 'Mark' at the end of line 7 has the same internal assonance as 'heart' at the end of line 9, so creating a sense of a perfect hit.

Language and imagery

A poem that compares a situation in an exaggerated way to something else is called 'a conceit'. 'Quickdraw' is a conceit that relies on the **extended metaphor** of a shoot-out for its effectiveness. The phones are 'like guns,

Glossary

pellet (l. 3) a bullet or piece of small shot; a small solid ball or mass

high noon (l. 10) the most advanced stage

calamity (l. 10) an event that brings terrible loss, lasting distress

Last Chance saloon (l. 11) a US bar indicating (literally) to customers that this was their final opportunity to drink alcohol before progressing to a county where alcohol was prohibited; (metaphor) a situation beyond which hope or good fortune will greatly diminish

Sheriff (l. 12) the chief law enforcement officer in a US county

Gary Cooper as Marshal Will Kane in the 1952 film *High Noon*

'I show the mobile/to the Sheriff,' — who do you think the Sheriff represents here? Another person? Or is Duffy herself the lone sheriff as in the film *High Noon*? Suggest more than one interpretation of this idea to get higher marks.

Pause for thought

The most famous user of silver bullets was 'The Lone Ranger', masked hero of the radio and television series from 1933 to 1969. He always arrived from nowhere, overcame evil and departed, leaving behind a silver bullet.

slung from the pockets on my hips' and the sharp voice at the other end of the phone is 'a pellet' that wounds. 'I twirl the phone' gives an image of a gunslinger spinning his pistol, before he fires his next shot. 'The trigger of my tongue' fires off the next hurtful remark — but misses, since it's 'wide of the mark'. Could this mean that what she says doesn't have the desired effect? Certainly the cutting response she receives does not miss, but has a devastating effect on the narrator.

And this is love, high noon, calamity, hard liquor
in the old Last Chance saloon (ll. 10, 11)

The list of metaphors here uses references to famous Western films. 'High noon' means the make or break part of the relationship, but also has connotations of the film *High Noon*, where a lone sheriff walks into the centre of town, steeling himself for a showdown — 'I'm all/alone.' (ll. 2, 3) The breakdown of this affair would have terrible repercussions for the narrator, but 'calamity' also suggests the Wild West heroine Calamity Jane, who, in the film of the same name, had a romance with gunfighter Wild Bill Hickok. 'Last Chance saloon' demonstrates the desperation at this stage of the quarrel and 'hard liquor' could be what cowboy and rejected lover alike might turn to.

Written in the **present tense,** so we can share in the action as it progresses, the **mood** of the poem changes as the argument grows cruel and destructive. The opening lines are almost jokey, yet when 'down on my knees' (l. 14) the opening swagger has turned to a 'fumble'. The receiver is now desperately upset. The **assonance** of the long 'ee' sound in the fourth stanza — 'concealed', 'reel', 'knees', 'read' — emphasises those long drawn-out moments when time seems to slow down.

The **repetition** in the last line:

Take this...
and this...and this...and this...and this...

fires out rhythmic kisses and although the little xs are sent by text, the effect is that of a passionate embrace between two lovers, making up after a quarrel. 'Silver bullets' finish the conceit at the end of the poem: we now use this term to mean something that provides an immediate solution to a problem, just like waving a magic wand. After all the distress of the disagreement, all is seemingly mended when they 'kiss and make up'. Once again we are reminded of a famous character of the Western genre, 'The Lone Ranger'.

Idea to consider

Duffy's poems often use a similar vocabulary to other famous love poets, yet she makes them contemporary with references to phones and their importance to us all in our everyday lives. Many relationships are made and broken by phone and text messages can wound, confuse, reassure and heal. In the poem 'Text' at the beginning of her anthology, *Rapture*, Duffy writes: 'I tend the mobile now/like an injured bird', a moving simile of how precious her new lover's words are to her and later, the couplet: '(I) look for your small xx,/feeling absurd.' Compare the line of kisses in 'Take this…/and this…and this …and this…' to 'your small xx' to appreciate fully the mood at the end of 'Quickdraw'.

Laura's poem 'The manhunt' by Simon Armitage

Context

The day after Remembrance Sunday, 2007, Channel 4 screened a documentary called *Forgotten Heroes: The Not Dead*, which told the stories of three soldiers, who had served in different wars and had returned home suffering from post-traumatic stress disorder (PTSD). The documentary explored how difficult it was for these damaged men to settle back into society, and the effect on their families. Armitage listened to each man's account of his devastating experience and refashioned the stories into poems to accompany the programme.

Eddie Beddoes, one of the featured soldiers, was attached to the United Nations peace-keeping force in Bosnia, and was still a teenager when he was shot in the neck and severely wounded. Discharged from hospital, he described himself as 'depressed, disfigured, disabled, useless'.

Although, at times, his wife Laura and his two young children suffered terribly from the changed man Eddie had become, Laura persevered to try to help him. 'The manhunt' is written using her account of the struggle to save her husband.

What happens?

The account is told in the first person from Eddie's wife, Laura's, point of view. When her husband first returns, they are obviously delighted to be together again, but it takes some time for him to allow his wife to touch the parts of his body so seriously disfigured and damaged by the bullet and his horrific experiences. It is not only the physical damage to his body that has not been repaired, but a great deal of psychological harm

> ### Glossary
>
> **intimate (l. 2)**
> very personal; private; can mean a sexual relationship
>
> **porcelain (l. 8)**
> ard, white ceramic; china
>
> **rudder (l. 10)**
> a hinged plate at the back of a boat or plane for guiding
>
> **struts (l. 13)**
> pieces of wood or metal that strengthen a framework
>
> **foetus (l. 19)**
> the unborn offspring of a human or animal

has embedded itself into the soldier's subconscious. Laura tries to imagine the extent of Eddie's suffering and has to admit that there are terrifying recollections 'buried deep in his mind' that he is unable to share. Only by accepting this can she learn to live with him.

Structure

Set out on the page in the shape of a human being, the poem suggests the outline of a victim of crime chalked on the ground — an interesting idea for a 'manhunt'. A human being has been reduced to an outline of the man he once was.

After the first three couplets of perfect rhyme, Armitage begins to use different techniques to link the two lines in each couplet. Parts of the wounded soldier's body are only just held together in the way the assonance is used in 'hold' and 'bone' (ll. 7, 8), 'thumb' and 'lung' (ll. 11, 12); the half-rhyme in 'attend' and 'blade' (ll. 9, 10) and 'hurt' and 'heart' (ll. 15, 16).

The tenth couplet, where the 'bullet had finally come to rest', returns to a complete rhyme, at the point where the cause of all the physical injuries has been located, before changing back to half rhymes and internal rhyme (ll. 23, 24) for the final couplets. The overall effect of these varied techniques seems to hold the whole poem together, while moving from one part of the soldier's body and mind to another. The relationship between husband and wife, once secure as the rhyming at the beginning of the poem, has been fractured by the horror of war. At the end of the poem the trauma that Eddie has witnessed seems 'closed' inside him. In trying to reach him and make him human again, Laura still, along with the rhyme, only comes 'close'.

Language and imagery

The first **metaphor** of the poem is its title. A dictionary definition of 'manhunt' gives 'an organised search for a wanted person, who has escaped or disappeared', therefore this is a very apt way of describing the wife's search for the husband she knew and loved before his terrible experiences in Bosnia. Metaphors are used extensively throughout the poem for each part of Eddie's damaged body.

- His facial scar is a 'frozen river' shiny and insensitive to feeling, along which his wife can run her finger.
- 'His lower jaw' has been shattered and hangs like a 'blown hinge'.

- The delicacy of bone and lung are emphasised with the use of 'porcelain' and 'parachute silk'.
- His ribs become rungs of a ladder that need strengthening.
- A pregnant woman sometimes has a 'scan' that shows the growing foetus inside her womb. On line 18 the wife imagines she can see the 'foetus' of metal in her husband's chest. Why do you think this image is used? Think about the way a baby grows. How could a bullet grow?

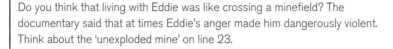

Pause for thought

Do you think that living with Eddie was like crossing a minefield? The documentary said that at times Eddie's anger made him dangerously violent. Think about the 'unexploded mine' on line 23.

Armitage, in the first 16 lines, selects adjectives to accompany the metaphors that could also be used to describe the ex-serviceman's physical and mental state: 'frozen', 'blown', 'damaged', 'fractured', 'punctured', 'grazed'.

The phrase 'only then' is often **repeated.** It stresses the length of time and patience required by Laura to try to touch and heal her husband. Gradually she seems to be making progress, and yet, at the end of the poem, she has to accept that she may never be able to restore Eddie to the human being he once was. 'I was a different person before I got shot,' Eddie said. 'I was a young lad, 19, out-going, happy, the world was my oyster.'

Ideas to consider

The words 'handle and hold' (l. 7) with their alliterative 'h' suggest the phrase used in a marriage service where the bride and groom both promise '**to have and to hold** from this day forward; for better, for worse…in sickness and in health, to love and to cherish, till death us do part'. Do you think Armitage intended this play on words?

Many young servicemen return from conflict having escaped death, but so damaged by their experiences that they cannot adapt to normal life. Armitage criticises the way they are neglected and the lack of support they receive from the British government. In another of his poems, entitled 'The not dead', he describes men like Eddie as:

creatures of different stripe - the awkward, unwanted, unlovable type -
haunted with fear and guilt,
wounded in spirit and mind.
So what shall we do with the not dead and all of his kind?

Poems from the English literary heritage
'Born yesterday' (for Sally Amis) by Philip Larkin

Context

Born in Coventry in 1922, Philip Larkin went to Oxford University to study English, before qualifying as a professional librarian. He worked as a librarian for the rest of his life, while publishing two novels and six anthologies of poetry that have given him a reputation as one of the foremost and best-loved twentieth-century poets. Having received many awards in recognition of his writing, especially in his later years, he was offered the chance to succeed Sir John Betjeman as Poet Laureate in 1984, but declined, not wanting to receive the media attention that such a title would bring. 'Born yesterday' was written in 1954, to celebrate the birth of Sally Amis, the daughter of Larkin's university acquaintance, novelist Kingsley Amis.

What happens?

Larkin addresses his poem to a newborn baby girl. He explains that his wishes for her future are different from the usual. He knows that other people will wish her beauty, purity and love, three well-meant attributes, and he even accepts that, if life holds these in store for the little girl, then she will be 'lucky'. His wish, however, is that she will grow up to be 'ordinary', with an average amount of talent and no exceptional beauty. He seems to feel that when a woman has extreme beauty or outstanding ability or intelligence, then that particular asset will prevent her leading a balanced and contented life. In the last five lines, he goes so far as to say that to gain delight and joy from life, she may need to be 'dull' — an adjective suggesting dreariness, lack of intelligence and interest. It does not matter, he suggests, as long as she enjoys life and he certainly wants her simply to catch a state of 'happiness'.

Structure

Twenty-four lines divide into two stanzas of ten and fourteen lines, the first describing the wishes of others, the second explaining why Larkin wishes the baby to 'be ordinary'. The poem does not have a rhyme scheme but there are two occasions where rhyme has been used. Lines 1 and 3 rhyme, with 'bud' and 'would', giving the impression of a formal speech at the beginning; the last couplet also rhymes to bring the presentation to an obvious end. This allows emphasis to be placed on the emotive word 'enthralled' before dropping, by **enjambement,** to the final line. Together the final lines have the feeling of a blessing.

Glossary

spring (l. 6) a stream of water flowing naturally from the earth; an origin, beginning

uncustomary (l. 16) uncommon, extraordinary

vigilant (l. 22) alert, watchful

enthralled (l. 24) filled with wonder and delight

The poem has a tight structure, with carefully considered short lines. The echo of sound created in the assonance of 'talents' (l. 4) and 'balance' (l. 7) assists in this.

Language and imagery

Although the subject of the poem — to celebrate the birth of a baby — is rather formal, Larkin throws in **informal** expressions such as 'Well' (l. 10) and 'In fact' (l. 20), which give a relaxed, personal feel, as though the lines are being delivered alongside the poet's train of thought. 'Not the usual stuff' seems an almost throwaway remark, yet it is carefully placed to express his lack of regard for stereotypical ideas about desirable female qualities. There is a sense of caring about this baby's future, written in the first person, rather than the anonymous verses found inside 'Congratulations on your new baby girl' cards.

The **metaphor** on line 1, gives a charming picture of a newborn baby. A flower begins life as a 'bud' ready to open out and show its full beauty as it grows; 'tightly-folded' suggests the curled-up position of a newborn child, who has only just left her foetal position in the womb. This image at the beginning prepares the reader for the idea that Larkin expects wonderful things to grow from the 'bud' and therefore his unusual wish for this child is all the more surprising. Another image: 'a spring/Of innocence and love' (ll. 6, 7) is presented in a dismissive tone. For a girl growing up in the 1950s and 1960s, life had to be lived realistically and Larkin knew this. Naivety (or lack of worldliness) does not fit with Larkin's opinion that for an 'enthralled/Catching of happiness' a woman needs to be 'vigilant'.

The **list** of adjectives in lines 21–23 builds up unexpectedly. Larkin says it is not easy to catch 'happiness' in life. It can so easily pass you by and needs skill, vigilance and flexibility if one is to achieve it. What do you think he means by 'unemphasised'? Look back at the adjectives he uses to explain his wishes for the baby — 'May you be ordinary' (l. 12), 'An average of talents' (l. 14), 'Nothing uncustomary' (l. 16) — 'unemphasised' probably suggests something similar to: easy, simple, natural. The delightful surprise at the end of this list is the word 'enthralled': at the end of all these uninspiring characteristics the one word sums up his hopes for Sally Amis. He wishes her a wonderful, enchanting life.

Ideas to consider

Larkin would probably have known well a poem called 'A prayer for my daughter', written in 1919 by the Irish poet W. B. Yeats. The following lines are from this poem.

Pause for thought

There is enormous pressure from the media nowadays for girls to look beautiful and much attention is given to physical appearance. Does an obsession with how you look 'pull you off your balance'?

May she be granted beauty and yet not
Beauty to make a stranger's eye distraught,
Or hers before a looking-glass, for such,
Being made beautiful overmuch,
Consider beauty a sufficient end,
Lose natural kindness and maybe
The heart-revealing intimacy
That chooses right, and never find a friend.

The idea that Yeats' daughter should be a 'flourishing hidden tree', instead of wishing her all the excitements and adventures expected for male children in 1919, has been criticised, particularly by people who feel Yeats was condemning his daughter to a dreary lifestyle. Do you think Larkin is expecting baby Sally to conform to the ideals of how women should behave in the second half of the twentieth century?

At the start of the twenty-first century girls are outperforming boys in their exam results, yet after education women tend to underperform compared to men. Do you think women are more content to settle for 'an average of talents'?

A classic fairy tale, *The Sleeping Beauty*, tells how, at a baby princess' christening party, her godmothers gave her wonderful presents such as beauty, intelligence and musical talent. A wicked fairy, angry at not receiving an invitation to the party, cast a spell on her that, when she was grown up, she would prick her finger on a spinning wheel and die. Larkin disagrees with 'the usual stuff' of well-wishers: he feels his gift of 'ordinari-ness' is what will make a woman happy. Perhaps some girls would view his wishes as more of a curse!

In 2000, when she was only 46, Sally Amis died. Unfortunately, she does not seem to have experienced an 'enthralled/Catching of happiness'. She had become an alcoholic and suffered from bouts of depression.

'Nettles' by Vernon Scannell

Context

Vernon Scannell was born in 1922 in Lincolnshire but moved around with his family before settling in Buckinghamshire. Leaving school when he was 14, he joined the army in 1940 and served in the Middle East and Normandy. The horrors of war had a profound effect on him, and the themes of war, suffering and death are often evident in the poetry of this Second World War poet. After five years in the army he deserted, later explaining that he had to escape from the conflict or lose his own humanity. Instead of serving a prison sentence, he was sent to a mental hospital from where he was soon discharged. He was delighted to have his freedom but felt guilty that other soldier colleagues were in prison for desertion or had died when he had survived.

Scannell loved boxing as well as literature and won championship titles at school and university. He gave up boxing as a young man and, in a poem called 'The loving game', makes it clear that love hurts more than any pain from such a violent sport. Love, in all its forms, is another theme that appears regularly in his poetry, often still influenced by his wartime experiences. He continued to write novels and collections of poetry up until his death in 2007.

What happens?

Told in the first person, this poem is autobiographical. The poet's three-year-old son accidentally falls into a patch of nettles and his parents comfort him in his distress. When he has stopped crying his father takes a billhook to the nettles and angrily cuts them all down, before burning them on a bonfire. Two weeks later new nettles have shot up in the same place and the father reflects on how his son would suffer again from the hurt and pain of life's experiences. He knows, however, that other anguishes would not be soothed so quickly or easily once the boy is older.

> ### Glossary
>
> **billhook (l. 9)**
> a tool with a curved or hooked blade at one end, for pruning and cutting
>
> **honed (l. 9)**
> sharpened with a hard stone
>
> **pyre (l. 13)**
> wood heaped for burning a dead body as a funeral rite

Structure

'Nettles' consists of one 16-line stanza, with a strong **regular metre** and rhyme scheme. The metre is iambic pentameter throughout, i.e. ten beats per line, with every second beat stressed:

> We so**oth**ed/him **till**/his **pain**/was **not**/so **raw**.

Scannell enjoyed using this rhythm, liking his poems to have a concise form. It seems to work particularly well in 'Nettles', which describes one short incident, dealt with and explained as a past recollection. The only line with any irregularity is line 10, which has an extra syllable on the end to emphasise the words 'with it'.

> 'And **went**/out**side**/and sla**sh**ed/in **fu**/ry ***with*** *it* '

Perhaps this adds to the 'fury' as the angry father tries to avenge his son's suffering, giving a sense of his aggressive strikes with the billhook.

The pattern of rhyming is also very regular — abab, cdcd, efef, ghgh — a basic pattern called cross rhyme, which, combined with occasional enjambement, gives a storytelling feel to the poem.

Language and imagery

The poem begins with a statement of fact in the way that somebody would tell a story. This **narrative** is helped along by expressions that give a **time sequence**: 'At last' (l. 8), 'And then' (l. 9), 'And then' (l. 12), 'in two weeks' (l. 14) and finally 'would often feel…again' (l. 16) looking forward into the future.

Scannell's anger towards the nettles is described using **military metaphors**. He questions the word 'bed', usually a comfortable place for relaxation, not for a patch of stabbing 'spears'. A 'regiment of spite' (l. 3) suggests a great number of nettles, all strictly disciplined and trained to attack. The father's intense response to the incident is suggested in the word 'spite'. When the 'fierce parade' (l. 11) of nettles has been cut down, he burns 'the fallen dead', (l. 13) an expression used to describe soldiers killed in battle. The nettles grow again, young fresh 'recruits', and the 'wounds' that Scannell knows his son will experience in later life will not be simply eased by soothing parental hugs.

The tenderness of the father towards the little boy is expressed in the metaphor of the nettle rash: 'White blisters beaded on his tender skin' (l. 6). This visual description also uses the **alliterative 'b'** sound to express contrast between the unpleasantness of the rash and a vulnerable child's soft skin. The same plosive 'b' returns in line 9: 'And then I took my **b**illhook, honed the **bl**ade' when a disgusted father prepares an angry revenge attack. The strong '**sp-**' in '**sp**ears' (l. 2) is repeated in '**sp**ite' on the next line and together they enforce the father's emotive response to his son's injuries.

Pause for thought

The last line is a father's reflection on the hurts, disappointments and pain of life. Parents can soothe the hurt of a three-year-old, but not the agonies of love and loss that most adults experience. Do you get the feeling that Scannell has had an unhappy life or is he a particularly sensitive person?

Key quotation

…those green spears,

That regiment of spite behind the shed:

Idea to consider

Scannell wrote a poem called 'The walking wounded' in which he describes the horror of war for the survivors. 'There was no splendour in that company' he writes, and finishes with the couplet:

The walking wounded still trudge down that lane
And when recalled they must bear arms again.

Can you see any similarity between the endings of the two poems?

'Sister Maude' by Christina Rossetti

Context

Christina Georgina Rossetti was born in 1830, in London, into a very artistic family. She was the youngest of four children, her brother being the poet and painter, Dante Gabriel Rossetti. She and her sister were devout

Anglicans and her Christianity is evident in her religious poetry. She became engaged at the age of 18, but broke off the engagement when her fiancé became a Roman Catholic. At 32 she fell in love again but refused to marry a man with no religious faith. Her poetry, as a result, often expresses a sad regret for lost love and an obsession with death. Since she suffered a great deal of ill health, she considered life to be a painful experience and considered death would be a happy release and a time of great joy and reunion with those loved and lost in life.

She died in 1894 and her brother edited her collected works in 1904, but the *Complete Poems* were not published until 1979. Today she is considered to be a major Victorian poet.

What happens?

Maude is jealous of her sister's lover. In the first verse she spies on the loving couple when they are together and then betrays them by telling her parents. The lover is dead in the second verse, and the narrator grieves for her beautiful lost young man. She tells her sister that she has pointlessly damned her eternal soul by the unkind betrayal: that the lover would never have considered Maude anyway. Her father is already in heaven, her mother will probably soon join him but her sister will never be allowed into heaven now, she says. There is a possibility that she and her lover might still be allowed access to heaven in the afterlife, but her sister Maude has sinned and she will have to live with guilt and in fear of death.

Structure

The poem is written in five stanzas, the first four having four lines and the fifth stanza six lines. The final two lines are perhaps added to give emphasis to the fate awaiting the jealous sister. Stanza five builds on the sentiments of stanza four, listing the family's rewards in heaven, before the final two-lined punishing outburst.

The second and fourth lines in each stanza **rhyme** cleanly in traditional poetic form, throwing emphasis on each final word. Look at the effectiveness of this technique on lines 12 and 13, where the sister's anger is directed towards the final pronoun:

> Though I had not been born at all,
> He'd never have looked at you.'

Most of the lines are end-stopped and there is a musical regular metre throughout, as the story enfolds, most lines consisting of four or three iambic feet:

> Oh **who** / but **Maude**, / my **sis**/ter **Maude**,
> Who **lurked** / to **spy** / and **peer** (ll. 3, 4)

Grade **booster**

Perhaps the most effective example of the power of a strong regular iambic metre is in the last line: 'Bide you with death and sin.' Everybody else may get to heaven but not 'you'.

Rossetti changes the metre occasionally, however, to stress a particular word.

- '**Cold** he lies' throws stress on the word 'cold' at the beginning of line 5 to emphasise suddenly the lover's death.
- Line 15 has a heavy iambic metre: 'But **sis**/ter **Maude** / shall **get** / no **sleep**', before line 16, disobeys this rhythmic pattern. It seems as though the line is shouted out as a child's tantrum, i.e. my sister Maude won't be able to rest in this life or the next — and it will serve her right.

Language

The speaker's **mood** is one of anger throughout. She switches between naming her betrayer as 'sister Maude' in the first two stanzas and the pronoun 'you', in stanza three, to accentuate her outrage. Returning to 'sister Maude' in the last two stanzas, she reserves the pronoun for the last line, where she can fully express her contempt for her interfering sibling

The **repetition** of 'Who told' with 'who but' and 'who' yet again in the first stanza highlights the speaker's exasperation that her jealous sister has dared to 'spy' on her and inform their parents. 'Cold he lies, as cold as stone' (l. 5) enforces the finality of death, while 'spared' and 'soul', repeated throughout lines 9 and 10, leave the reader in no doubt about the poet's religious convictions that the only way to a blissful afterlife is to live a sin-free life on earth. 'Sleep' repeated in stanza four symbolises the peace that is given to those people who have led honourable, virtuous lives. The illicit lover is named as 'my dear' in lines 2 and 19. Although his moral reputation is tarnished once the scandal of the affair has been exposed, the speaker still hopes that she and her lover might be allowed into paradise. Sister Maude, however, she condemns eternally.

The **interjection** 'oh' is found on line 3 and again on line 21, each time expressing surprise that her own sister should have betrayed her.

Alongside the repetition, Rossetti uses **alliteration** for dramatic effect. The harshness of death is described in stanza two with the repeated letter 'c'. The dead lover has 'clotted curls' and is the 'comeliest corpse'. Perhaps for a short while the anger changes to a sense of loss, yet there is an unusual emphasis on the physical description of the dead body. The Victorians had an almost fanatical obsession with death, believing in bodily resurrection, and devised elaborate rituals to deal with it. The corpse remained in the family home for family and friends to view until the burial. The afterlife was expected to be wondrous, literally a shining kingdom where an angel would wear 'a golden gown' and 'a crown' would

Pause for thought

What do you think 'clotted curls' means? A cluster or mass of curls or thick with blood? How has the young man died?

reward you for your goodness on earth. The internal rhyme on line 18 adds to this glorious image.

The **old-fashioned terminology** dates the poem in the nineteenth century. 'My dear' is no longer a common term for a lover and the name 'Maude' has dropped out of fashion. Line 11 would now translate as 'if I had not been born at all' and 'bide' is an archaic verb, found mainly in poetry and hymn lyrics now. The imperative form 'Bide you' with its plosive 'b' strengthens the final threat.

Ideas to consider

Prince Albert, the husband of Queen Victoria, died in 1861, when he was only 42 years old. The queen mourned her husband for the rest of her long life. Rossetti's collection of poetry containing 'Sister Maude' was published in 1862. Do you think Rossetti could have had the royal couple in mind in stanza two?

From 1859 until 1870, Rossetti was a voluntary worker at Highgate Penitentiary, a charity set up by the church to reform women, particularly prostitutes, whose lifestyles were considered immoral. Victorians had a strict set of moral standards and a very narrow attitude towards sex. Any woman who had sexual relationships out of marriage was considered a 'fallen woman'. Rossetti was particularly interested in the effect women had on each other in all-women communities and during this time wrote 'Sister Maude'.

'Sonnet 116' by William Shakespeare

Context

William Shakespeare, the Bard of Avon, was born at Stratford-upon-Avon in 1564 and died in 1616. As well as his famous plays, he wrote a collection of 154 sonnets, dealing with the themes of love, beauty, politics and death. The first 17 sonnets address a young man, trying to persuade him to get married and pass his beauty on to his children; sonnets 18–126 are also written to a 'fair youth', but now express the poet's love for him; numbers 127–52 are love poems written to the poet's mistress. The 'fair youth' in the first 126 sonnets remains unnamed. Some people are convinced that the loving, romantic language suggests a homosexual relationship; others argue that the relationship is purely platonic; a third group believe Shakespeare could even be writing to his son. Sonnet 116 is one of the most famous of the

Glossary

impediments (l. 2) hindrances or obstructions

bark (l. 7) ship (archaic)

sickle (l. 10) the cutting tool carried by the Grim Reaper (Death)

bears it out (l. 12) endures, stays faithful

doom (l. 12) Judgement Day

writ (l. 14) wrote (archaic)

sonnets, the ideal definition of love that it provides being regularly quoted and included in anthologies of love poetry.

What happens?

This sonnet presents Shakespeare's opinions of genuine love, which has no flaws whatsoever. It never changes, is 'never shaken', cannot fade with the passing of time and outlives death itself. 'The marriage of true minds' has all these qualities, he argues, and any form of love that is otherwise cannot be love.

Structure

This sonnet obeys all the rules of the traditional Elizabethan sonnet. Written within a tightly-structured 14-line framework, it consists of three quatrains (four-line stanzas) and a rhyming couplet. 'Prove' and 'love' (ll. 3, 14) nowadays are eye rhymes i.e. they look as though they rhyme but are pronounced differently. However, their pronunciation when Shakespeare wrote the poem would probably have made them full rhymes. Each four lines rhyme with the regular pattern of abab, cdcd, efef, then gg for the last couplet.

The iambic pentameter rhythm remains constant throughout the poem. It is possible to read the poem as though it is a glorious meditation on the powers of love, stressing whichever syllables you wish in order to give your own personal interpretation. In Shakespeare's time, however, it was expected that iambic metre followed a consistent format and in doing so Shakespeare is able to put across his own mood and feelings. Compare version A of lines 1 and 2 (where the stressed syllables are in bold font):

A

'**Let** me / **not** to / the **marr**/iage of / **true minds**

Ad **mit** / im **ped**/i ments. / **Love** is / not **love**…'

to version B, where the stresses follow the iambic pattern:

B

'Let **me** / not **to** / the **marr**/iage of / **true minds**

Ad **mit** / im **ped**/i **ments**. / Love **is** / not **love**…'

Suddenly the sonnet has a completely different tone and, therefore, meaning. Version A has a romantic feel, putting heavy emphasis on the emotive words 'true minds' and repeating 'love' as in dreamy thoughtfulness; version B, however, has the feel of somebody replying in the middle of a conversation, as though he is speaking in his own defence: 'Don't accuse *me* of not knowing what true love is. This is what it really is…'

Whereas we should feel free to read and interpret poetry as we wish, it is very interesting to consider the tone in which it was probably written in the 1590s, when Shakespeare was in his thirties.

Although line 12 has the word 'even', suggesting two syllables instead of 'e'en', people who have studied Shakespeare's sonnets insist it should be pronounced as one syllable — 'een'. Take care also to read 'fixed' on line 5 as two syllables, i.e. 'fix-ed', to keep the regular metre.

Language and imagery

The first four lines argue that there should be no obstacles to two people loving each other. The **metaphorical** 'marriage' combined with 'impediments' has clear echoes of the wording of the marriage ceremony. In the Elizabethan wedding ceremony the priest would ask the bride and groom: 'I require and charge you that if either of you do know of any impediment, why ye may not be lawfully joined together in matrimony, that ye confess it.' A 'marriage of true minds', rather than bodies, suggests a union that is not physical, but platonic and idealistic, the adjective 'true' meaning faithful and unchanging. This theme of constancy is then developed in lines 3 and 4: love does not change when circumstances change; it does not switch direction for the sake of convenience.

The second quatrain, lines 5–8, states what love is, in contrast to what it is not. Another **metaphor** is used — 'an ever fixed mark/That looks on tempests and is never shaken.' Elizabethan sailors, with no lighthouses to guide them, would watch for prominent landmarks — church spires or a group of rocks, sometimes beacons lit at the port entrances — to work out their position at sea. These would always be in the same place — they could be trusted to remain fixed. Storms would have no effect on them whatsoever, in the way real love would not be damaged by disagreements and hard times.

Another effective image is that of genuine love being a guiding star for lost sailors, probably meaning the Pole star, which seems to remain static, while the other stars move around it. The stars were a great mystery in the sixteenth century. It was not known what they were made of or what made them shine, thus their 'worth' was 'unknown', although they could measure their 'height' from the earth. In the same way, Shakespeare argues, love is an unknown quantity that can be neither understood nor described, but we should be guided by it.

The third quatrain (ll. 9–12) introduces the idea of time **personified**. Love is not the fool of time. Time alters most things and the beauty of youth has to change, when Father Time, or The Grim Reaper, cuts down our lives and years with his 'bending sickle'. But, if love remains

Grade *booster*

Read the last line with the iambic stress on the word 'no' and you might hear Shakespeare's tone of voice as if he is saying 'I dare you to argue with me'.

Key quotation

It is the star to every wandering bark,

constant, then hours and weeks seem short and time is powerless, even to death or the end of the world (Judgement Day).

For the final couplet, Shakespeare needs to put forward an especially clever argument to make his case. 'If I'm mistaken,' he sums up, 'and you can prove that I don't understand what true love is, then I'm not a writer and nobody has ever been in love!' When he wrote this poem he was convinced that he was in love, and he was clearly a very successful poet and playwright, so he disproves any argument anybody might present.

Ideas to consider

What tone do you think Shakespeare would use to read the last couplet? Is he boasting, angry, sarcastic, smug, confident? Perhaps he is daring somebody to argue with him — or you may still want to believe it to be a celebration of eternal love, which is why this poem is often read at weddings.

In Shakespeare's time the word 'fool' (l. 9) would have more than one connotation. As well as meaning somebody who is easily made to appear ridiculous or simply an idiot, it was also the name of a professional clown (a jester), employed by a king or nobleman, to entertain. It was not a comfortable job as fools could be easily dismissed or cruelly punished.

Compare 'Love's not Time's fool' (l. 9) to the first line of 'Hour' by Duffy: 'Love's time's beggar.' Both poets are writing a love sonnet, but their arguments are different when they compare the relationship between time and love.

'Sonnet 43' by Elizabeth Barrett Browning

Context

Elizabeth Barrett was born in 1806 in Durham, the eldest of 12 children. The Barrett family had lived in Jamaica for hundreds of years, where, part Creole, they had owned sugar plantations and relied on slave labour. Elizabeth's parents returned to England before their children were born and she was educated at home, developing a great love of literature from an early age. She began writing poetry at the age of 12, but was never healthy, suffering from a lung ailment and spinal injury. As she grew older she became active in church and missionary society activities and was an enthusiastic, committed Christian.

Elizabeth continued to publish her work, but the next 16 years seem to have been very unhappy ones: her mother died; Mr Barrett sold his plantations and moved his younger children to Jamaica to help with the family's estates (although Elizabeth was bitterly opposed to slavery); her brother drowned in a sailing accident; and Barrett became a reclusive invalid.

In 1844 she produced a collection of poetry admired by the poet, Robert Browning, who wrote to her, and their romance began. Some 574 letters and 20 months later, they eloped to Italy, since Elizabeth's harsh, domineering father refused to allow them to marry. They had a son and Elizabeth's collection of sonnets entitled *Sonnets from the Portuguese* was published in 1850. These sonnets, including 'Sonnet 43', had been written in secret and dedicated to Robert Browning, before their marriage. Today they are still considered by many to be her best work. One of the leading female poets of the Romantic movement, Barrett Browning died in Florence in 1861.

What happens?

'Sonnet 43' is the most passionate and emotional of the 44-sonnet sequence. The poet reflects on the magnitude of her love for her husband-to-be, listing the qualities of her secret love. First she announces that when she searches spiritually for answers about life's purpose and the way to achieve fully God's divine love and protection, then her love for him has all the answers. Moving on from the spiritually sublime, she accepts that her adoration can be a simple part of their everyday lives together. Her love is given willingly, in the way that people decide to fight for freedom; her love is given simply, in the way that the virtuous do not expect to be praised. She recalls strong emotions of suffering, which she felt as an innocent trusting child and then recollects her childlike enthusiasm for saints in all their holiness. The poem finishes with an exclamation that all her life's experiences have culminated in this present love, which, God willing, will even be strengthened after death.

Structure

This sonnet is an Italian, or Petrarchan, sonnet, i.e. fourteen lines divided into two sets of six and eight with ten syllables on each line. Sonnets are traditional forms for love poetry and usually have a strict iambic pentameter rhythm, rather like a heartbeat — dee **dum**, dee **dum**, dee **dum**, dee **dum**, dee **dum** — but Barrett Browning could be breaking the rules on the first line:

> **How** do / I **love** / thee? **Let** / me **count** / the **ways**

By accenting 'How' instead of the second word 'do' the poet would emphasise her thoughts on the different aspects of her love, instead of the methods she uses to demonstrate her passion. It is as though she were thinking aloud, preparing in her delight to count on her fingers. You may,

Pause for thought

The poet claims that she could not love Robert Browning more than she does: 'I love thee to the breadth and depth and height/My soul can reach…' (ll. 2, 3) yet on the last line she hopes 'I shall but love thee better after death'. How do you think her religious faith is affecting her feelings here?

however, feel that all the iambic rules are obeyed and the word 'do' is stressed. In this case she would seem to be saying 'I really *do* love you so much'.

Barrett Browning knew the conventions of the Italian sonnet, in fact she was translating Petrarch's sonnets into English while writing her own, yet she chose to break the rules in places. Perhaps she felt that her life was governed by too many rules: an over-strict father who did not want her to marry; poor health that denied her an active life — and, therefore, it was desirable to break a few rules for the purpose of expressing her secret love.

The iambic pentameter rhythm changes in other places, perhaps to prevent a sing-song quality that might detract from the content. At times, the rhythm soothes, as in line 6. Elsewhere it changes dramatically. After the regularity of line 11: 'I l**ove** / thee **with** / the **breath**', line 12 gushes out with '**Smiles**, **tears** / of **all** / my **life**' disrupting the iambic metre again in her overenthusiastic state.

Enjambement also moves the poem away from traditional end-stopped form when Elizabeth Barrett (as she would have been when this was written) sometimes allows her emotions to carry her across lines, as though lacking sufficient control in her proclamation.

The rhyme scheme follows the Italian sonnet rules with abba cddc for the first octave (eight lines) and the remaining sestet (six lines) cdcdcd. 'Faith' at the end of line 10 is not a full rhyme with 'breath' and 'death' but the final consonants are the same. The 'breath/...of all my life' rhymes then with 'death' to surprise us at the end.

The first octet lists the four ways in which Barrett Browning professes her love: spiritually; materially — 'at the level of everyday's/Most quiet need'; willingly; genuinely. The final sestet first compares her present emotions to her childhood passions, when she loved with the innocent faith of a child; and moves on with the exclamation that her husband-to-be is now the recipient of all her strong emotions; and concludes in the hope that they will be together in love in the future.

Language and imagery

'How do I love thee?' is asked at the beginning and answered repeatedly throughout the poem. The **repetition** of 'I love thee' adds pace to the poem and enforces the joyous mood of a woman who is sure of her feelings but is not allowed to broadcast them. Her father's refusal to condone the relationship makes the celebration of this spiritual love very romantic. This is probably why this sonnet is such a well-known love poem.

The comparisons for how Barrett Browning loves her fellow poet refer to traditional moral or religious issues of Victorian times. She does not use Valentine-type images of red roses, full moons, twinkling stars, (although references to 'sun and candlelight' are used to suggest day and night). Instead she packs her sonnet with morally themed words such as 'Being', 'Grace', 'Right', 'Praise', 'faith', 'saints' — all words deeply rooted in her strict religious upbringing and concepts of which the high-minded Victorians would approve. Note their importance in the way some are written with capital letters.

The language is obviously archaic with its frequent use of 'thee', and the final line sounds very formal. The sentiments, however, are similar to love poems and songs across the centuries, whether Barrett Browning writes 'I shall but love thee better after death' or Whitney Houston sings 'I will always love you'.

'The farmer's bride' by Charlotte Mew

Context

Charlotte Mew was born in 1869 in London. When her architect father died, she and her sister and mother were left in poverty. Two of her siblings suffered from mental illness and Mew grew up terrified of inheriting such illness herself. Her personal life suffered a series of setbacks when the two female writers with whom she fell in love rejected her affection. Her sexuality is not addressed directly in her poetry — many presume she was a 'chaste' lesbian, on account of Victorian morality codes. It is known, however, that she refused to marry for fear of passing insanity to any children she might have.

Mew grew up at the end of Victorian times and died in the reign of George V. Throughout her lifespan the Women's Suffrage Movement was actively trying to achieve votes for women and the campaign accelerated when Mew was in her thirties. She also lived through the First World War and ideas such as death, loss and insanity are major themes in her poetry, along with unrequited love. Most of her poems were published in 1916 in the one anthology: *The Farmer's Bride*, after which she wrote very little. Her sister died in 1927 and Mew took her own life in 1928.

What happens?

The dramatic monologue is narrated in the persona of a farmer who explains how he decided to marry a girl, who was 'too young maybe' and then neglected her due to the demands of harvesting. Frightened of her new husband, the young wife runs away in the autumn, but she is chased

Glossary

bide (l. 3) stay at home

woo (l. 3) make love to

fay (l. 8) fairy

Fall (l. 9) autumn

abed (l. 11) in bed

beseech (l. 25) beg

stall (l. 27) stable, pen for animals

leveret (l. 30) young hare

rime (l. 38) coating of ice

betwixt (l. 44) between

down (l. 44) fine, soft hair on the skin; soft, fine feathers

across the countryside by a search party, brought back to the farm and locked in. Three years later, still a prisoner in her own home, the girl is content amongst the animals, but will not speak to men around the farm, in particular her husband. The seasons pass, and as Christmas approaches again, the farmer regrets there are no children from the marriage. At the end of the poem the girl still sleeps alone in the attic above the farmer's bedroom and the farmer's sexual longings intensify.

Structure

Mew narrates her poem in five stanzas of unequal length. **End rhymes** run through the whole poem, the pattern changing with each stanza. She seems particularly fond of **rhyming couplets** when trying to put across the passions of the speaker: 'Too young maybe — but more's to do/At harvest-time than bide and woo.'

There are also examples of **internal rhyme** to keep the musical quality of the story. Lines 13 and 15 hold 'Lying' and 'flying' with 'stay away' on line 24. With many examples of near rhyme, assonance and consonance it is clear that Mew's enjoyment of sound is more important than following poetic rhyme tradition.

The **metre** also changes throughout. The dominant rhythm is iambic tetrameter, i.e. four feet of two beats (eight syllables) with the second beat emphasised, e.g. 'She **does** / the **work** / a **bout** / the **house'** yet there are also iambic pentameter lines and an assortment of other metres for effect. Look at line 30: '**Shy** as a / **lev** er et, / **swift** as he', where the sudden unusual 3 x 3 foot (dactylic) metre sounds like the quick antics of a wild hare. The iambic rhythms give us the story, but the changes surprise and entertain.

Language and imagery

The poem is full of **dramatic irony**. The farmer tells his story in detail, concealing nothing, yet it is clear to the reader that he has little under-standing of the situation. He does not understand his bride's feelings and he cannot articulate his own. This comes across as a series of images and **similes** related to the farmer's life in the countryside. He describes his wife 'flying like a hare' (l. 15), 'like a mouse' (l. 21), 'shy as a leveret' (l. 30), 'straight and slight as a young larch tree' (l. 31), 'sweet as the first wild violets' (l. 32) — she is even covered in 'soft young down' (ll. 44, 45). There is a definite tenderness in the way he describes his 'wild' young wife, yet the verbs that describe his treatment of her: 'chased', 'caught', 'fetched her home', 'turned the key upon her, fast' demonstrate his inability to treat her gently. Instead he rounds her up like an escaped animal and fences her in. The farm images also serve to show the young woman's love of animals, her affinity with the natural world and her fear 'Of love…and all things human'.

The arrival and passing of **the seasons**, important times on the countryside calendar, seems to emphasise the farmer's growing despair. He married in the summer, was too busy at harvest-time 'to bide and woo' and his wife ran away in 'the Fall'. Three years later, as Christmas approaches, the lonely farmer still sleeps alone. The berries may 'redden up' but the **colours** of the landscape in stanza six are bleak and uncomforting: 'oaks are brown', 'blue smoke rises to the low gray sky', 'the black earth is spread white with rime'.

The **country dialect** fits the storytelling rhythm in early lines such as 'One night, in the Fall, she runned away' (l. 9) and 'Out 'mong the sheep, her be, they said' (l. 10). It is interesting that the farmer seems to lose his dialect in the later stanzas. The poet often went to stay with her grandfather, who was a farmer on the Isle of Wight. Perhaps that is where she found the dialect and idea for this story.

At times the **sense of immediacy** is heightened through the farmer's exclamations: *'I've* hardly heard her speak at all' (l. 29) he complains. And again on line 33 when he laments: 'But what to me?' His wife's wild beauty is so evident around the farm, yet her fear of her husband and, it would seem, men in general, leave him unable to tolerate the situation. At the end of the poem he is distraught at the thought of her beauty lying untouched in the attic above him. 'Oh, my God!' he exclaims and his cry is heartfelt. The **repetitions** of the final words convey not only repressed sexual desire, but perhaps hint at approaching madness, something Mew was very frightened that she might have inherited in her own life:

A startled leveret

> …the down,
> The soft young down of her; the brown,
> The brown of her — her eyes, her hair, her hair!

Ideas to consider

The young bride could be suffering from an illness called androphobia, which means she is terrified of men. On the other hand, she may just be frightened of the farmer himself and the way he has treated her. Line 13 'Lying awake with her wide brown stare' could suggest she is frightened about the sexual side of the marriage.

What do you think Mew is saying about arranged marriages? 'Three Summers since I chose a maid' (l. 1) does sound as though the farmer has gone to market to buy a cow, rather than marrying for mutual love. He spends no time with the young girl helping her to adjust to married life and it is obvious that he wanted a woman who would 'do the work about the house'.

Do you feel sorry for either of the characters in this unhappy marriage? Perhaps our feelings for the farmer change at different times in his narration. Select two separate quotations that evoke different responses when you read them.

'To his coy mistress' by Andrew Marvell

Context

Andrew Marvell was born in 1624. When he was three years old, he moved with his family to Hull in Yorkshire. Having graduated from Cambridge University, he travelled widely in his early twenties throughout Europe, before returning to England to work as a private tutor during the English Civil War. In 1659 he entered politics and was best known during his lifetime as a politician rather than as a great poet. 'To his coy mistress' was discovered and published in 1681, shortly after Marvell's death in 1678.

Marvell is one of a group of seventeenth-century poets called the metaphysical poets. Their witty poetry involves the use of their intellectual and scholarly skills, where they play word games and express strong feelings related to their experiences of life. An extended metaphor is often used with other surprising images that shock and delight the reader.

What happens?

A young man tries to seduce a young woman. First, he argues persuasively that it would be wonderful to have endless amounts of time to get to know each other and praise each other — before they begin a physical relationship. Unfortunately, he continues, human beings soon age and lose their beauty and all that is left are death and

Glossary

coy (title) shy and quiet — but still flirtatious

mistress (title) in Renaissance England calling a woman 'mistress' usually meant a female friend, not a sexual partner

vegetable (l. 11) probably suggests 'able to spread quickly'

vault (l. 26) an underground burial chamber

hue (l. 33) the colour of a healthy (rosy) complexion

transpires (l. 35) breathes moisture through the skin

amorous (l. 38) showing love and sexual desire towards another

languish (l. 40) to lose strength; to pine away in longing

slow-chapped (l. 40) slowly chewing

strife (l. 43) angry or violent struggle

thorough (l. 44) archaic form of 'through'

the cold grave. Therefore, he concludes, let us enjoy a sexual relationship while we're young. Let us not waste any more precious time.

Structure

The logical three-part argument fits neatly into the three stanzas. The metre is iambic tetrameter, i.e. four feet of two beats with the stress on the second:

> An **hun**/dred **years** / should **go** / to **praise**
> Thine **eyes** / and **on** / thy **fore** / head **gaze**

Look at line 44: 'Thorough the iron gates of life.' Do you think Marvell, in his passionate appeal, suddenly stresses the first syllable, breaking the metre pattern?

Rhyming couplets are an ideal choice of rhyme pattern for an argument. In stanza one they present a light, teasing tone — (their speed and bounce suggest they should not be taken seriously perhaps?) In stanza two the tone changes. The argument is moved along by warning that 'time's winged chariot' means they are ageing quickly and they can do nothing about it. The frightening images cancel out all the fantasising of stanza one, ending with a cold frightening couplet:

> The grave's a fine and private place
> But none, I think, do there embrace. (ll. 31, 32).

With the opening words of the final stanza the tone changes again. 'Now therefore' (l. 33) turns the argument back to the poet's conclusion — 'Now let us sport us while we may' (l. 37) the seducer encourages lustfully.

There are many examples of **enjambement**, where the pace is almost breathless and sounding like somebody delivering a one-sided speech.

Language

Stanza one contains (subjunctive) **verbs** such as 'Had', 'were', 'would' and 'should', all wishful verbs, gently trying to persuade the woman of the young man's honourable intentions. He really 'would' be prepared to wait for a physical relationship with her — if it 'were' possible. Compare the mood of these verbs to those in stanza three. 'Let us sport us', he forcibly suggests; 'Let us roll' and 'tear our pleasures with rough strife.' These imperative verbs are vigorous and persuasive. He ends with the line 'We will make [the sun] run' — an enthusiastic statement that allows no argument.

The long **alliterative** 'l' sounds in 'long love's day' (l. 4) stretch the phrase to make it sound delightfully lazy. '**Th**irty **th**ousand' years seem a very long time with the repeated 'th' sound. Marvell understates the horrors of the grave by calling it a '**p**rivate **p**lace' and the repetitive use

Grade **booster**

Comment on the effect that Marvell achieves by the continuing rhyme and rhythm throughout the poem. Perhaps there is a hint that Marvell (in the persona of a young man) is enjoying the argument, although not taking it seriously. To raise your marks, provide alternative interpretations of the poet's purpose.

of the 's' sound in stanza three: '**s**trength', '**s**weetness', '**s**trife', leading up to 'though we cannot make our **s**un/**s**tand **s**till' in the final lines, seems to enforce the speaker's seductive skills.

Hyperbole in the first stanza tries to convince the 'mistress' of the vast amounts of time the young man would be prepared to spend flirting with his desirable girlfriend, before even considering consummating their love. The sacred Indian river Ganges and the busy Humber estuary in Yorkshire, where Marvell grew up, are continents apart and so could the lovers remain, if they had 'world enough, and time'. He could spend the whole of the historical timeline between Noah's flood in the Bible and the time when Jewish people would be prepared to convert to Christianity, (in other words, from the beginning of the world to the end), just telling her how wonderful she is. He would leave the adoration of her heart until the last, since that was where her passion could be found.

Imagery

The second stanza picks up the sense of 'If only I could, then I would' and insists immediately 'but I can't' with the opening lines:

> But at my back I always hear
> Time's wingèd chariot hurrying near:

Time is now **personified** as a chariot driver chasing all mortals towards their deaths at the finishing post. In Greek mythology, Apollo, the sun God, flies daily around the world, shortening lives with the passing of each day. Fear and dread now enter the poem in a succession of **metaphors** and terrifying images.

- 'Deserts of vast eternity' suggests dry barrenness where nothing will grow — no fertility and definitely no place for enjoyable lustful pursuits.
- A 'marble vault' is a cold tomb with no passion, warmth or feeling. 'My echoing song' of love would just bounce futilely off the unresponsive walls.
- 'Worms shall try that long-preserved virginity' is a shocking image, where only putrefaction would invade the corpse. 'Why stay a virgin just for the worms to enjoy you!' the speaker asks. 'My fiery passion will end up just as ashes.'

The images of death and decay are suddenly replaced in stanza three by descriptions of youth and its beauty. The comparison is very effective after the scariness of stanza two. 'Now therefore,' the young man pleads, having reached the conclusion of his reasoning, 'let us sport us while we may' and devour time 'like amorous birds of prey'. The **simile** compares the way humans allow time gradually to eat away at their youth, to birds

Pause for thought

There is no mention of an afterlife in the poem, although religion was thought to be very important in the seventeenth century. Why do you think Marvell, a clergyman's son, decides not to mention the idea of heaven?

of prey who 'devour' their recent kill with no idea of what is right or wrong — they just enjoy the present.

Lines 41–44 contain two enthusiastic **metaphors** about making love. The image of a cannonball, breaking through 'iron gates', suggests the physical sexual act, while also insinuating the breaking down of 'long-preserved virginity'.

The poem ends with an image of life, returning to the sun god, who will have to 'run' to keep up with such worldly pleasures. There is a sense of delight at the end that Marvell's persona has proved his argument and the lady therefore should now be prepared to give up her virginity. On the other hand, it is highly likely that the poet realises his poem is just a clever word game: loss of honour in Marvell's age would deny a woman any chance of marrying a man of high status or wealth.

Ideas to consider

'Carpe diem' (meaning 'seize the day' — live for the present, since we have no control over the future) is a sombre warning that we are all going to die and that death is no joke. Does this mean that we should all enjoy our lives while we can? Is 'Well, we'll be dead soon' a good argument for sexual relationships at any time, or should we live by moral or religious beliefs to preserve our 'honour' (l. 29)? Could Marvell be warning the reader of how a young man might try to persuade and flatter a young woman?

The word 'quaint' (l. 29) seems to be referring back to the 'coyness' in the title. Both words suggest a pleasing quality, but there is also the added sense of being old-fashioned and unusual in an attractive way. Do you think Marvell is mocking the young woman's wish to remain a virgin, or simply teasing her? Perhaps he is pretending to compliment her?

The seventeenth century was a time when the British Empire was expanding rapidly. When Marvell wrote about the Ganges, he introduced the exotic East into his poetry. Explorers such as Christopher Columbus were discovering new lands and India, with its valuable rubies (believed to preserve virginity), would seem a very exciting place.

Types of conflict

- Which poems explore conflict in war?
- Which poems explore the feelings of people caught up in conflict?
- Which poems express conflict in the poets' opinions?

All 15 poems in the 'Conflict' section of your anthology have been chosen because in some way they deal with the same theme. The word 'conflict' has many interpretations, therefore it is a wide and interesting theme to write about. Below are some dictionary definitions of 'conflict':

When used as a noun:

1 a battle or war
2 a struggle or clash between two opposing groups or individuals
3 a state of disagreement and disharmony between persons or ideas or interests
4 the problem in any piece of literature

When used as a verb:

1 to fail to be in agreement; to oppose or clash
2 to fight
3 to go against the rules or laws

To help you understand the many ways in which the 'Conflict' poems can be compared, different aspects of the theme are put into categories here. A poet has a purpose to convey and your personal interpretations of the opinions and ideas of a poet are what matter in the exam. It is important that you recognise the conflict in the poets' minds as well as the settings or events described in the poems. Keep your mind wide open when dealing with the theme and make sure you recognise that the poems often belong in more than one aspect of conflict.

Conflict in war

'The charge of the Light Brigade' recounts the tragic events at the Battle of Balaclava in 1854, when conflicting instructions led to the slaughter of hundreds of men, who knew they were beaten before they advanced towards the enemy. Tennyson calls them the 'noble six hundred' yet repeats the ambiguous line 'All the world wondered', which surely suggests his own doubts about the ineptitude of those in command. Other poets have doubts about the futility of war, many of them writing about the First World War, 1914–1918. Their feelings often conflict with the patriotic mood of their country and its government. Hughes' soldier in 'Bayonet charge' 'runs/ Listening…for the reason/Of his still running' and the persona speaking in Owen's 'Futility' questions sadly the purpose of conflict when young healthy men, 'so dear-achieved' are so quickly sacrificed.

The horror of the waste of young lives is also presented in 'Mametz Wood' where, many years after the 1916 battle, the bodies of the dead soldiers are discovered with their arms linked as though caught up in a dance of death. 'Come on, come back', on the other hand, leaps into the future and envisages the dehumanising processes used in chemical warfare as a damaged girl, deprived of her memory and identity, will never 'come back'.

> **Pause for thought** ⏸
>
> Each day news reports bring us up-to-date coverage of conflicts being fought in different parts of the world. We witness as if at first hand the violence and suffering and devastating loss of life. In contemporary times it is thought acceptable to question whether a country should engage in foreign conflicts; during Victorian times it would have been considered unpatriotic; in the First World War it was because of the poetry written by soldiers on the front line that the public became aware of the painful misery of war.

Caught up in conflict

Some poets tell their own stories, narrating their experiences when conflict came to them. Ciaran Carson in 'Belfast Confetti' cannot make sense of the chaos caused when he's caught up in street riots. 'I know this labyrinth so well', he exclaims, yet all he finds are dead ends and a 'fusillade of question marks'. 'The yellow palm' describes the devastation of the beautiful city of Baghdad and the suffering of the Iraqi civilians when attacked by bombing raids and 'the slow and silver caravan' of a cruise missile. 'Poppies', on the other hand, brings the suffering into the home, describing the fluctuating emotions and memories of a dead soldier's mother, who listens at the war memorial 'hoping to hear/[his] playground voice catching on the wind'.

The setting for Hardi's 1979 autobiographical memory is also Iraq. The Kurdish refugees, persecuted and driven out of Iraq five years previously are returning from Iran to their homeland and the poet remembers her lack of understanding at the 'check-in' point. 'The chain was removed to let us through', Hardi remembers, yet conflict for the Kurds would remain in whichever country they tried to settle.

The extract from Armitage's 'Out of the blue' describes a recent attack that we all witnessed on our television screens. The voice of an imaginary trader in the World Trade Center plays out the 'appalling' inner turmoil as the trapped civilian realises he has become a victim of somebody else's conflict.

> Grade **booster** ❗
>
> Those contemporary poets who write from a personal perspective are able to describe their feelings in convincing detail. To achieve high marks, explain how the poets' own involvement helps you to explore their attitude to conflict and to empathise with them.

Conflict in opinion

Reports in Western newspapers detailing the attacks on the Twin Towers have always named the perpetrators as terrorists. Dharker examines the word 'terrorist' in 'The right word'. She struggles to find a description for somebody who is willing to commit violent acts because of their passionate beliefs. While she does not condone any organised system of intimidation, she does accept that anybody's son with his 'hand too steady' and his 'eyes too hard' could become involved in a minority cause. Agard in 'Flag' complains that flag-waving 'brings a nation to its knees' and Cummings mocks the way patriotism is the reason why so many rushed into death 'like lions to the roaring slaughter', not stopping to consider that 'the voice of liberty' should allow them to speak up for what they think is right.

Review your learning

(Answers to these quick questions are given online)

① Which poems refer to conflict in the First World War?

② In which two poems is Iraq the setting for the conflict?

③ Which word does Dharker explore?

Longer questions

④ 'Hawk roosting' by Ted Hughes does not seem to fit into any of the three conflict categories. Write a paragraph explaining why you think it has been included in the theme of 'Conflict'.

⑤ Continue Table 1 so that all 15 'Conflict' poems are listed down the left-hand side and tick the appropriate box(es). For some poems you will find you need to tick more than one box for the same poem.

More interactive questions and answers online.

Table 1

	Conflict in war	Caught up in conflict	Conflict in opinion
Flag			
Bayonet charge			
The falling leaves			

Types of relationship

- Which poems explore family relationships?
- Which poems explore sex in relationships?
- Which poems express romance in relationships?

Dictionary definitions of the word relationship are as follows:

1 the state of being connected or related
2 association by blood or marriage
3 the mutual dealings, connections, or feelings that exist between two people, organisations, countries etc.
4 an emotional or sexual affair or liaison

All 15 poems in the 'Relationships' section of your anthology have been chosen with the same theme in mind. Because we are all human beings, we need to interact with other people, and our developing relationships with others take us on emotional journeys through the whole of our lives.

Pause for thought

Have you ever written poetry?

It is not important that you know exactly how the poets felt when writing the poems but what is important is that you try to engage with the poems in order to have your own interpretations. You may not be old enough to understand how parents feel towards their children. It is unlikely that you have yet met 'the love of your life' and you will not yet have experienced a long-term love affair. However, you may be able to relate to feelings about your mother, father, brother or sister and you will soon be at an age when you could be having to make decisions about sexual relationships. Whatever your experiences regarding relationships, you will probably already understand the whole range of emotions, from longing, excitement and joy to jealousy, anger and pain, so use these feelings alongside the poets' language and skills to produce your personal responses.

Not all the poems fit neatly into just one of the following categories. 'Ghazal', for example, by Khalvati, uses a form of poetry that traditionally deals with only spiritual longing, yet her modern version would seem to also desire physical intimacy. Duffy's 'Hour' describes lovers in 'a grass ditch', yet the richness of their feelings for each other makes them 'million-aires' in love, not just sexual partners.

Family relationships

'Harmonium' and 'Nettles' both use an autobiographical incident to explore the father and son relationship. While the voice in 'Harmonium' is that of the adult son recognising his father is growing old and not knowing how to respond to his father's anxiety, the younger father is the speaker in 'Nettles', who knows he will not always be able to comfort his son from life's 'sharp wounds'. Nichols looks back with great affection and praises her generous, yet selfless, mother; the speaker in 'Sister Maude' has no respect, on the other hand, for her jealous sister and angrily curses her for her betrayal.

Other emotions towards family members are expressed in 'Brothers' and 'Manhunt': Forster remembers his unkind treatment of his trusting younger brother; Laura, the wife of a soldier severely wounded in Bosnia, desperately tries to love and understand her husband after his traumatic experiences. Larkin writes 'Born yesterday' for a friend's baby daughter, wishing her a 'Catching of happiness' in her 'ordinary' relationships.

Sex in a relationship

'To his coy mistress' is a well-known seventeenth-century poem of seduction. Marvell's narrator may flatter his girlfriend in the first stanza, insisting that she deserves thousands of years of adoration, yet he is really arguing cleverly that there is no time to lose, in order to get her to yield to a physical relationship with him. In contrast, Mew's farmer has no persuasive words, no subtlety at all, when dealing with his young frightened wife. Having spent his life looking after the needs of his animals, he is unable, like his wife, to deal with 'love…and all things human'.

Paris is an extremely romantic city, yet the confessed anger at the way he has been treated in a previous relationship soon evaporates when Fenton's persona recognises the physical attractions of another woman. The 'sleazy/Old hotel room' perhaps suggests an illicit relationship, making it all the more exciting, whereas the 'cuckoo spit' and 'grass at your ear' of Duffy's poem 'Hour' make the 'grass ditch' seem uncomfortable to anybody other than people wanting to escape from the eyes of the world to be together for a short time.

Romance in a relationship

'No chandelier or spotlight see you better lit', Duffy writes in 'Hour'. Anywhere can seem romantic when two people in love 'find an hour together' and romance and sex often co-exist in a fulfilling relationship.

The romance in a relationship does seem to fade when the arguments begin, as 'Quickdraw' demonstrates, yet sex is not always necessary for romance to flourish. In 'Sonnet 43' Barrett loves 'with the breath, smiles, tears, of all (her) life', while she secretly writes to Robert Browning before they eventually elope to marry. Shakespeare, in 'Sonnet 116', argues there is nothing that can obstruct 'a marriage of true minds'. 'Love is not love/ Which alters when it alteration finds' is not a line Marvell's young persona is likely to have written to his 'coy mistress'.

Review your learning

(Answers to these quick questions are given online)

1 Which poems explore the parent/child relationship?

2 Which love poems use the sonnet form?

3 In which poem does a wife explore her husband's body to try to understand his suffering?

Longer questions

4 Write a paragraph explaining why you think 'Born yesterday' has been included in the 'Relationships' cluster.

5 Continue Table 2 so that all 15 'Relationship' poems are listed down the left-hand side and tick the appropriate box(es). For some poems you will find you need to tick more than one box for the same poem.

More interactive questions and answers online.

Table 2

	Family relationships	Sex in relationships	Romance in relationships
Praise song for my mother			
Ghazal			
To his coy mistress			

Comparing poems

- Is it worth doing a plan for my response?
- Which aspects of the poem should I compare?
- Which are the most important aspects to compare?

The examination for Unit 2 'Poetry across Time' lasts 1 hour 15 minutes and is divided into two sections. In Section B you have to answer in 30 minutes a question on a poem you have not read before (see p. 94; Section A requires you to **compare** two poems in 45 minutes.

In Section A, all students have to select one question (from a choice of two) from the poetry theme studied, for example, 'Conflict' *or* 'Relationships'. One poem will be named and the question will ask you to **compare** this poem with any other of your choice from the same cluster. The foundation-tier question will give an extra reminder, in two bullet points.

> Remember to compare:
> - what the conflicts/relationships/feelings are
> - how the conflicts/relationships/feelings are presented

How do I time-manage my response?

Divide your time as follows:

- 5 minutes — write a plan for the named poem and your chosen poem
- 35 minutes — compare the two poems
- 5 minutes — read through your response to check what you have written and make any last minute changes

So how do you make sure that you compare? If you write about two poems without comparing them, then you are not going to gain the marks your understanding deserves, even if you show excellent appreciation of each poem.

The Assessment Objective that the examiners are looking for wants you to compare and contrast the different ways in which poems express meaning and how they do this. Try dividing this objective into four parts for your response.

A four-part plan for your response

1 **What** do I think the poet is saying in poem A?
  How does this **compare** with what the poet is saying in poem B?

2 **Why** does poet A feel like this? Does the poet have a purpose? What is the tone/mood of the poem? Does this change?

How does this **compare** with poet B's feelings and purpose?

3 **How** does the poet express himself/herself by the techniques used?

Compare each technique that you write about in poem A with a similar or different technique in poem B. Go to the literature guides website to download tables that will help you compare poetic techniques.

(This is a very important part of your response, so try to analyse a number of techniques in detail. Select the outstanding techniques used in the poems and compare and contrast them, making sure you analyse their effect on the reader.)

4 How do I feel about these two poems?

Compare your personal response, either expressing a preference and saying why, or explaining the different/similar effect of each poem on your own emotions. See the **Grade focus** below.

Grade *focus*

Compare these grade C and grade A responses to understand how to make sure that your response finishes in an impressive way.

'I enjoyed both of these poems, but I prefer "Praise song" to "Born yesterday". I like the way Grace Nichols says her mother was always "replenishing, replenishing" because it sounds as though she was always there to look after her daughter.'

This answer expresses a preference, gives quotation and explains why — grade C.

'Both of these poems gave me plenty to think about, but I think I prefer "Praise song". The repetition of "replenishing, replenishing" suggests a constant giving of love and filling up with all the needs of a growing child. "Born yesterday" suggests that girls would be happier if they were "dull" and I don't agree with this. Nichols' mother was very special to her and not at all "ordinary".'

This answer expresses a preference, gives quotation and then compares to the first poem with another relevant quotation that links both poems — grade A.

A quick framework for your plan

Table 3 gives an example of how you could plan your response, using the four-part plan. This is a response to the question:

Compare the ideas and attitudes shown to war in 'The yellow palm' by Robert Minhinnick and one other poem in the Conflict cluster.

Table 3 Plan for comparing poems

	Yellow palm	Light Brigade
What	**Baghdad 1998** **civilians suffering**	**1854** **doomed — cavalry men** **'blunder'd'**
Why?	**personal viewpoint + quotes** **shocked — beautiful place/ destruction**	**amazed** **admires?** **certain death** **'wondered'** **'not to reason why'**
How? 1	**dactylic — galloping + q**	**song-type rhythm —** **contrast with horror**
2	**(Make quick notes on second technique)**	**(Compare/contrast second technique)**
3	**(Make quick notes on third technique)**	**(Compare/contrast third technique)**
How do I feel?	**long time ago**	**heartbreaking — beggar child** **+ q**

Using your plan to write your response

Imagine Table 3 is the plan you have quickly devised. Below is just an example of how you could use it for your response. Notice the comparison words in capital letters, which help to make sure you compare.

1 The 'WHAT are the poets saying?' section

In 'The yellow palm' Minhinnick describes his experiences as he walks down a street in Baghdad in 1998. Iraq is being violently attacked by the US and all the senses of the poet are alert to the sufferings of the civilians caught up in the war. 'The charge of the Light Brigade' **ALSO** describes violent warfare where many lives are lost, but the doomed cavalrymen lost their lives in 1854, because 'Some one had blunder'd'.

(Keep this concise, since the next two sections are the most important.)

2 The 'WHY are they saying this?' section

Minhinnick writes 'As I made my way down Palestine Street' **to ensure the reader shares** the sights and sounds of Baghdad **from the poet's personal viewpoint**. In six stanzas the sufferings of the Iraqi people and all the terrors of the bombing campaign are detailed. Women form the funeral cortège for a man who has 'breathed a poison gas'; there is 'blood on the walls' of the mosque where people have gone to pray peacefully; a sinister Cruise missile seeks out its next target. **The poet seems to be shocked** that in such a beautiful place there can be so much destruction and loss of life.

Tennyson is **SIMILARLY** shocked by loss of life, but he wrote 'The Light Brigade' **out of amazement** and probably **admiration** that soldiers would be prepared to ride into certain death. As Poet Laureate at the time he would want to praise the bravery of the 'Noble six hundred' yet his ambiguous line 'All the world wondered' suggests that he could not believe that such a serious mistake could be made by those with the responsibility for soldiers whose duty was 'not to reason why'.

(Make sure you have compared the poems before you move on.)

3 HOW? (comparison of techniques section)

Tennyson uses a very heavy **dactylic metre** throughout his poem to give the effect of the galloping horses as they charge forward: 'Half a league, half a league.' Whenever the lines end with a word that rhymes with 'hundred' — 'blunder'd', 'thunder'd' — then the line is clipped and the effect is one of a roaring, relentless charge. 'The yellow palm', **ON THE OTHER HAND**, has a **song-type rhythm**, but it is just as effective since the gentleness of the iambic metre when describing 'the muezzin's eyes' which were 'wild with his despair' contrasts with the actual horror of the situation and seems to make it all the more distressing.

(You should carry on now to compare two other techniques (numbered 2 and 3 on the plan) — perhaps **repetition** in each poem — or **metaphors** — there are lots to choose from, but aim to compare and contrast two or three.)

4 The 'HOW DO I FEEL?' section

I enjoy reading 'The Light Brigade' aloud with its galloping rhythm. Since the Crimean War was over so long ago, the incident is interesting, but no longer particularly upsetting. **IN COMPARISON** Minhinnick's poem is heartbreaking. The contrasting image of the smiling 'beggar child' and the missile programmed to kill is frightening and it saddens me that war today still causes so much innocent suffering.

(Keep this section short.)

Grade **booster**

Make sure you integrate short quotations from both poems throughout all the sections of your response to support your analyses.

(Answers to these quick questions are given online)

1. Which are the two main aspects of the poems that need to be compared?
2. What kinds of word will make sure I compare?
3. How many techniques should I compare?

Longer questions

4. Compare how the relationship between parent and child is shown in 'Praise song for my mother' and one other poem from 'Relationships'.
5. How does Ted Hughes' attitude to conflict in 'Bayonet charge' compare to the views expressed by another poem in the 'Conflict' cluster?

More interactive questions and answers online.

Writing about an unseen poem

In Unit 2 Section B both higher-tier and foundation-tier candidates must answer a question on an unseen poem. This involves reading the poem and structuring your answer in 30 minutes. The higher-tier question will have one part; the foundation-tier question will be in two parts. Here are examples of the kinds of question you will be asked:

Higher tier

What do you think the poet is saying and **how** does he (or she) present his (or her) ideas?

Foundation tier

What do you think the speaker feels?
How does he (or she) present his (or her) feelings?

Can you see that both tiers are asking the same question? The plan for your answer needs to contain the same four-part sections that you used to answer Section A of Unit 2. The WHAT? and WHY? sections will help you answer the first part of the question; the HOW? and HOW DO I FEEL? sections will make sure you answer the second part of the question.

Simply changing the poet's words into your own words will not gain you many marks. You must pick out quotations to explain the poet's purpose and select techniques the poet uses to get his ideas across to you. Your personal response is also important.

Tackling the assessments

- **How do I choose which question to answer?**
- **How should I plan my response?**
- **What does PEE mean?**

If your teacher has chosen for you to study Unit 2 'Poetry across time', then you will be answering questions about poetry in an external examination. The poetry questions are worth 35% of your total English literature grade, with 25% on Section A and 10% for Section B, so you need to impress the examiners. It is not only important that you know the poems in your chosen cluster well, it is also vital that you know what the examiners are looking for. (Check the Assessment Objectives on p. 102.)

Choosing the question

In Section A you will be given a choice of two questions from each themed cluster, so choose carefully. Do not automatically choose the question where a poem you like is the named poem. There is the possibility that you will be able to choose that poem as your own choice in the other question. Instead, look carefully at what the question is asking you to do, before you decide. Open your anthology and look down the list of poems you have studied in your cluster. Then you can easily consider all your other choices, with the details of the question in mind.

Planning your answer in exam conditions

When you have chosen your question, highlight the key words by circling them. Don't worry about marking the anthology — it is your exam and the materials are there for you to mark as you wish.

1 Copy the main part of the question onto the top of your planning page.
2 In freehand draw your three vertical columns and write the titles of the two poems along the top. (See Table 3 on p. 92.)
3 Draw four horizontal lines to make your grid, ready to fill in with What?, Why?, How?, How do I feel?

Grade *booster*

It is a good idea to make a quick list of comparison words, somewhere on your planning page, to help you to remember to use them.

4 Now make the notes for your plan, keeping an eye on the key words in the question on top. Note how you don't need many words to remind you of your ideas. Shorten titles and just write q for quotation.

5 As you write your response, cross off the words in your plan as you transfer the ideas into your writing. This way you will be able to structure your answer and make sure you don't repeat yourself.

Starting to write

The examiners are not expecting you to produce a piece of writing like a formal essay. They are looking to see whether you can meet the Assessment Objectives.

Time is short, so don't waste it on a dull introduction. Attack the question straightaway. Look at the three examples of response openings below. Imagine the question asks:

> Compare the attitudes to love in 'Sonnet 116' to one other poem in the 'Relationships' cluster.

A I am going to compare 'Sonnet 116' by William Shakespeare to 'The manhunt' by Simon Armitage. They both deal with the theme of relationships, but there are similarities and differences.

B 'Sonnet 116' and 'The manhunt' were written 300 years apart, yet they both share the theme of love. Shakespeare's sonnet, however, says love is never 'shaken', whereas the wife who narrates 'The manhunt' must find it very difficult at times to continue to love somebody who has changed so much.

C 'Sonnet 116', written at the beginning of the seventeenth century, insists that true love does not 'alter when it alteration finds'. 'The manhunt' also explores love, but in a challenging modern-day situation, where a wife struggles to find the man she once loved, when horrific experiences in war-torn Bosnia have psychologically changed the man she married.

Notice how A has not yet started to analyse the two poems, whereas B and C start immediately to answer the 'What?' section — and already use relevant quotation. This leaves more time to explore poets' purposes and techniques, the two most important areas.

How do I achieve a good grade?

Using PEE

An important skill you need to practise in order to develop your ideas and achieve a good grade is PEE. The three parts, which your teacher has probably explained to you, are as follows:

- Point — make your point.
- Evidence — back it up with words quoted from the poem.
- Explanation — give detail about why this works well.

Grade *focus*

Compare these examples of how to use PEE at grade C and grade A, using Andrew Forster's poem 'Brothers'.

Grade C

The narrator doesn't want to look after his little brother for the afternoon (**Point**). He says he was 'saddled' with him and that his brother was wearing a 'ridiculous tank-top' (**Evidence**). These words really show that he'd been told to look after his brother against his wishes. He felt his brother's knitted top wasn't fashionable and showed up the two older boys, who thought they were grown-up (**Explanation**).

Grade A

From the first word, Forster expresses dissatisfaction with the responsibility he has been given (**Point**). The strong metric emphasis on the colloquial 'Saddled' ensures the reader is left in no doubt about an older boy's reluctance to look after his six-year-old brother 'for the afternoon' (**Evidence**). At the proud ages of nine and ten, Forster and his friend are too 'cool' to be spotted with a child 'in a ridiculous tank top', who dares to 'skip' and 'windmill', as they 'amble' and 'stroll'. Together they smugly and secretly acknowledge that they have to tolerate the annoying youngster, until the opportunity arises to free themselves of him. This quick decision was to remain in Forster's memory even when he was an adult, probably due to the guilt he later felt (**Explanation**).

It is always a good idea to make sure your **Explanation** is longer and more detailed than the other two parts. Notice how each response answers all **PEE** requirements, but the A grade response has more detail and shows that the candidate develops the idea made in the **Point**.

Achieving a grade C in foundation tier

To achieve a grade C in foundation tier, your answer needs to show the following:

- a thoughtful response to the poet's ideas and techniques with quotations to support your opinions
- an appreciation of how the poet's ideas and techniques affect the reader
- a developed and detailed comparison of two poems, in terms of ideas, techniques and their effect on the reader

Achieving a grade A in higher tier

To achieve a grade A in higher tier, your answer needs to show that:

- you can perceptively explore the poems, with close analysis of detail to support your interpretations
- you can judge the quality of the poets' ideas, themes and techniques (language, structure, form) by convincingly explaining their effect on the reader

- you can compare the ideas and techniques used in two poems by critical analysis
- you can integrate detail into your comparison which demonstrates full engagement with the poems

Examples of grade C and grade A* responses to 'Relationships' poems

In the extracts below the students are comparing the endings of Duffy's poem 'Hour' and 'Ghazal' by Khalvati.

Grade C response

At the end of 'Hour' Duffy writes that 'Time hates love, wants love poor'. She probably means that time is the enemy of love, because when you are in love you want to spend lots of time with each other and time passes too quickly. The last line goes on to say 'But love spins gold, gold, gold from straw', which is saying that if you're in love you can never be poor because love makes you feel rich. In comparison the poet in 'Ghazal' says she would also be rich in love if only the person she is addressing would love her back. She says (with a clever play at the end on her name Mimi) that she would be 'twice the me' if her love could be returned.

This answer fully supports each point with a quotation and a thoughtful explanation, and the same aspect of each poem (the ending) is compared. However, most of this response tries to put the poet's words into the candidate's own words. The response could be improved by:
- exploring the language in more detail
- explaining why the language is effective
- linking these ideas with other words and ideas in the poems

Grade A* response

At the end of 'Hour' Duffy writes 'Time hates love, wants love poor'. The personification of vindictive Time shows the writer's resentment that she has so little time to spend with her lover. It's as though Time is scheming to keep them apart. She wins the contest, however, at the beginning of the last line, asserting with the word 'But', that 'love spins gold, gold, gold from straw'. Time may try to impoverish love, she exclaims joyfully, but it can't succeed, since love makes everything wonderful. The repetition of 'gold' could emphasise her conviction that the delights of the love affair will continue. The last couplet of 'Ghazal', on the other hand, lacks the conviction that love will continue. Khalvati still seems to be trying to persuade her intended lover that their relationship would be enchanting. 'If only half the world you are to me' may be a clever wordplay on the name Mimi, but it could also suggest that she's willing to compromise on the amount of love returned to her.

This response shows close analysis of detail and clear appreciation of both poets' intentions through the language they use. Alternative interpretation is also suggested.

Examples of grade C and grade A* responses to 'Conflict' poems

In the extracts below, the students compare the opening stanzas of 'The right word' by Imtiaz Dharker and 'Hawk roosting' by Ted Hughes.

Grade C response

Dharker's poem begins with 'Outside the door/lurking in the shadows'. This is a very scary start, because it's dark outside and the word 'lurking' could mean that the person could be dangerous, because he's hanging around and you can't see his face. When the third line says he 'is a terrorist' it makes it seem even more terrifying since terrorists are known to kill innocent people. 'Hawk roosting' begins by describing a hawk in a frightening way as well. The bird's 'hooked head and hooked feet' show he is specially made to hunt and the last line says he is dreaming about 'perfect kills', which is a cold and cruel thing to dream about.

This answer fully supports each point with a quotation and a thoughtful explanation; also the same aspect of each poem (the beginning) is compared. The response could be improved by:
● exploring the language in more detail to explain its effectiveness
● explaining how the language links to language used elsewhere in the poems
● analysing the poets' purposes and feelings in their use of language

Grade A* response

'The right word' sets out from the start to terrify the reader. The first word 'Outside' is repeated in each stanza, perhaps to offer some reassurance, since the shadowy figure with the changing title remains on the other side of the door, until the final stanza when he 'steps in'. Yet it also suggests fear, since the visible threat is so very close. 'Lurking in the shadows' presents a sinister introduction to 'a terrorist', the emotive name alone conjuring up instant connections to the murder of innocent people in planes, on trains and in tower blocks. Hughes introduces 'Hawk roosting' in a sinister way, by writing the poem in the persona of a hawk. The predatory creature is frightening in its 'inaction' and the repetition of 'hooked' immediately portrays the bird as an exceptional killing machine. The arrogant admittance that 'perfect kills' are rehearsed 'in sleep' shows a creature designed by 'the whole of Creation' to 'sit in the top of the wood' like a god and survey his inferior kingdom.

This response shows detailed and developed analysis of language and clear appreciation of both poets' intentions.

> **Grade _booster_**
>
> Analysing and comparing the effect of the language used in the opening and closing lines of poems could help you raise your grade.

Spelling and punctuation

To gain a high grade you need to express yourself clearly and accurately. It is important that your writing is fluent and focused on the question. Make sure you always read through what you have written to ensure your spelling and punctuation are correct.

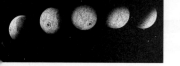

Practice questions

Use the questions below to practise your exam response. Don't forget to start with a plan.

Foundation tier

1 Compare how war is shown in 'The falling leaves' and in one other poem from 'Conflict'.
Remember to compare:
- the ideas about war in the poems
- how war is presented in the poems

2 Compare how a poet's attitude to conflict is shown in 'Flag' and in one other poem from 'Conflict'.
Remember to compare:
- the attitudes in the poem
- how the attitudes are presented

3 Compare the way family relationships are shown in 'Sister Maude' and in one other poem from 'Relationships'.
Remember to compare:
- what the relationships are like
- how the relationships are presented

4 Compare the way ideas and feelings about relationships with other people are expressed in 'In Paris with you' and in one other poem from 'Relationships'.
Remember to compare:
- what the ideas and feelings are
- how the ideas and feelings are presented

Higher tier

1 Compare how poets use language to express their feelings about conflict in 'Belfast confetti' and one other poem from 'Conflict'.

2 Compare how attitudes to war are presented in 'next to of course god america' and one other poem from 'Conflict'.

3 Compare how one person's feelings for another person are presented in 'Quickdraw' and one other poem.

4 Compare the emotions expressed in Sonnet 43 with any other poem in 'Relationships' where the poet has strong feelings about love.

Unit 5: 'Exploring poetry'

If your teacher has chosen for you to respond to poetry as a Controlled Assessment task, then you will have more time to write about and compare the poetry you have studied.

You will be given a question based on poetry linked by one particular aspect: theme and ideas, or genre and form. The poems you choose to compare must be from the English (Welsh or Irish) literary heritage as well as by contemporary poets.

The Assessment Objectives are exactly the same, whether you respond to poetry in an external exam or in controlled conditions in the classroom. The main difference between the two assessment requirements is that you have up to four hours for Unit 5 and are advised to write up to 2,000 words. This means that your response will be more wide ranging and developed than is possible in a shorter examination.

Sample 'Controlled Assessment' questions

1 Explore the variety of attitudes to relationships that can be seen in a range of contemporary and English literary heritage poems.

2 Compare the ways the sonnet form of poetry is used by English literary heritage poets and contemporary poets.

3 Which poems from the *Moon on the Tides* anthology do you think are the most inventive? You must consider poems from the literary heritage as well as contemporary poems.

4 Choose two English literary heritage poems and two contemporary poems on the theme of conflict for a series of A3 posters. Explain what photographic images you would choose as a border for each poem and relate all the images to the language of the chosen poems.

Grade *booster*

To organise your Controlled Assessment make sure you write a plan. The 'Plan for comparing poems' can be adapted for any number of poems.

Assessment Objectives and skills

- Which three Assessment Objectives will the examiners be looking for?
- What do these Assessment Objectives mean?
- What will I have to do in Section A and Section B of the poetry exam?

What are Assessment Objectives?

The Assessment Objectives are what an examiner looks for when deciding what mark to give you. Make sure you include *all* the following in your responses to poetry.

AO1

Respond to poems critically and imaginatively; select and evaluate relevant textual detail to illustrate and support interpretations.

This means that you must answer in a detailed way that shows you can imagine what the poets are trying to say and why they have written the poems. Pick out words, groups of words or lines and quote them to back up your ideas.

AO2

Explain how language, structure and form contribute to poets' presentation of ideas, themes and settings.

This means that you must write about the choices the poets make:

- in the words they use (techniques such as metaphors, repetition, alliteration, ambiguity)
- in the way they shape their poems (are the lines/stanzas long or short; regular/irregular; beginnings/endings?)
- in the form of poem they choose (free verse, sonnet, dramatic monologue, ghazal, ballad?)

Can you explain why you think the poet has chosen to write the poem using these particular techniques? How do they link to the poet's ideas?

AO3

Make comparisons and explain links between texts, evaluating writers' different ways of expressing meaning and achieving effects.

This means that, when you are writing about more than one poem, you should point out **similarities and differences** in the poets' ideas and the techniques they use to express their ideas and feelings, making sure you suggest the effects of the poets' choices on the reader.

Where will you need to show you understand the Assessment Objectives?

Unit 2 choice

If your teacher has chosen for you to answer poetry questions in an **external examination** then you need to demonstrate all the Assessment Objectives.

Section A

You have to compare one poem selected by the examiner with another poem of your choice from the same themed cluster. **Demonstrate AO1, AO2, AO3.**

Section B

You will be given an unseen poem to read, followed by a compulsory question about that poem. **Demonstrate AO1 and AO2.**

Unit 5 choice

If your teacher has chosen for you to show your understanding of poetry as a **controlled assessment**, then you need to respond to **AO1, AO2** and **AO3** throughout. Make sure you respond to all three assessment objectives equally.

Sample responses

Below are sample extracts from responses to help you to understand how you can demonstrate the required skills. Remember, for a full response you must compare poets' purposes and ideas as well as poetic techniques and their effects on the reader.

Conflict

Writing about poets' purposes and ideas

> 1 Compare how attitudes to conflict are shown in 'The charge of the Light Brigade' and one other poem from 'Conflict'.

C-grade response

Tennyson wrote 'The charge of the Light Brigade' when he read in the newspaper about the heroic defeat. He seems to have thought the cavalrymen were very brave to charge forward although they knew they were riding into a valley with the enemy on all sides. **1** He says there were cannon 'to right of them/cannon to left of them/cannon in front of them', yet they rode 'boldly' and 'well'. **2** He must have admired them to write this. **3**

He also writes: 'Honour the charge they made,/Honour the Light Brigade' at the end, so that people reading about the battle will also feel that the soldiers deserve to be honoured. **4** In Victorian times it was very important that you should be prepared to sacrifice your life for your Queen and your country, so back home in England people would really admire the 'noble six hundred' and their bravery. **5**

The soldier in 'Bayonet charge' felt just as patriotic as the cavalrymen when he went out to fight in the First World War. **6** Hughes writes about 'The patriotic tear that had brimmed in his eye/Sweating like molten iron from the centre of his chest'. **7** I think this means that when he was caught up in the rifle fire he was so terrified that he didn't think of anything except getting out of the battle alive. **8** The last stanza says 'King, honour, human dignity, etcetera/Dropped like luxuries in a yelling alarm'. When he was really scared he didn't care anymore about fighting for his King. He wanted to get out of 'that blue crackling air'. **9** He was carrying a heavy bayonet which was useless and you can tell he is terrified of dying like the 'yellow hare that rolled like a flame'. **10** The Light Brigade cavalrymen in their uniforms would also be useless against the cannons, but 'Cossack and Russian/reel'd from the sabre stroke' and they continued to fight. **11**

1 Makes point about poet's purpose

2 Backs point up with quotations

3 Explanation undeveloped

4 Interprets poet's purpose with quotation detail

5 Appreciates effect of language on readers, but again doesn't develop the explanation

6 Compares ideas between poems

7 Supports point with relevant quotation

8 Begins to interpret point made, but no analysis of language

9 Point, quotation and explanation

10 Develops point with quotation, but no explanation or analysis

11 Compares ideas with quotation detail

A*-grade response

Tennyson wrote 'The charge of the Light Brigade' as a personal response, upon reading details of the heroic defeat in the newspaper. The way in which the valiant cavalrymen were prepared to ride into almost certain death obviously intrigued and amazed the poet laureate. **1** 'Some one had blunder'd' he writes, and 'Charge for the guns! he said', so although no names are mentioned, he makes it clear to the British public, that the 'noble six hundred' had been sacrificed unnecessarily by those in command. **2** The use of the exclamation mark alone demonstrates Tennyson's disbelief at the apparent ineptitude. **3**

The cavalrymen, of course, would not even have considered refusing to obey the foolish command to advance. 'Theirs but to do and die' suggests their purpose in the Crimean War was to go out and prove their loyalty to the Crown and if this meant death — then so be it — theirs was 'not to reason why'. **4** Tennyson sets out to 'honour' this loyalty, while questioning whether 'the valley of death' should have been allowed to claim the lives of so many young men: 'All the world wondered' he repeats, to emphasise his amazement at their gallantry, while ambiguously suggesting that such an unbelievably idiotic tactic would be questioned worldwide. **5**

The soldier in 'Bayonet charge', over 50 years later, would also have set out from England with a 'patriotic tear' in his eye. Yet caught up in the terror of a battle with 'bullets smacking the belly out of the air' he instantly forgets all the 'luxuries' of 'King' and 'honour', which had previously fuelled his enthusiasm to fight the enemy and to become a hero. **6** The second stanza explores the sudden realisation that he had totally misunderstood what 'raw' conflict would be like. Now he was 'running like a man who has jumped up in the dark'. The phrase 'in the dark', suggesting his confusion, leads him to question 'the reason of his still running'. In desperation he 'plunges' forward in terror, caring only for his own survival. **7** The idea of a need to survive doesn't even enter the heads of the six hundred who also 'plunged in the battery smoke'. Hand to hand combat, whether by bayonet or sabre, would be ineffective against rifles and cannons as the soldier in the WW1 trenches and cavalrymen were all aware, yet the soldier wishes to 'get out of that blue crackling air' while the cavalrymen rode 'boldly and well' into the 'jaws of Death'. **8**

1 Insightful response to poet's purpose

2 Close analysis of language and effect on reader

3 Evaluates poet's use of punctuation

4 Convincing interpretation of idea

5 Developed evaluation of poet's purpose and opinions

6 Insightful comparison of ideas with details

7 Close analysis of detail to support interpretation

8 Close analysis of detail to support interpretation

Writing about poetic techniques and their effect on the reader

> **2** Compare how the poets express their opinions about war in 'Mametz Wood' and one other poem from 'Conflict'.

C-grade response

The pieces of the soldiers' skeletons are all described as though they are very precious: 'the china plate of a shoulder blade, the relic of a finger'. Sheers uses these metaphors to show his respect for the men who had died at the battle of Mametz Wood. **1** He describes a skull as a 'blown and broken bird's egg'. I think this makes you feel sad, because the skull would be empty just like a bird's egg where the baby bird would have died, because it had been blown out. **2** The simile 'like a wound working a foreign body to the surface of the skin' works really well. In the same way as a splinter works its way out of your skin, the earth has pushed the dead soldiers onto the surface of the field. **3**

Mametz Wood is written in one long stanza. This could be because the poem is all about one main idea, which is to describe the soldiers who had all been buried together 'a broken mosaic of bone linked arm in arm'. **4**

In contrast to this, 'Futility' has two seven line stanzas. I think this could be because the mood of the poem changes. In the first stanza the speaker seems to believe that if the body of the dead soldier is moved 'into the sun' it will warm up and he will wake up. He can't believe this won't work because 'Always it woke him'. In the second stanza, however, the speaker realises that nothing will bring back the young man from the dead. He grieves for the waste of a young life, saying 'Was it for this the clay grew tall?' **5**

A*-grade response

Sheers' respect for 'the wasted young' is obvious in the language he uses. The farmers 'tended the land back into itself' gives the first hint that the ground held something precious. **1** The ploughed up 'relics' are described metaphorically: 'the china plate of a shoulder blade...the blown/and broken bird's egg of a skull'. A china plate is delicate and very easily broken, just as the lives of the young men had been sacrificed. The visual picture of the broken, empty skull is extremely poignant: in the way that a young bird is not allowed to live its life, once the egg is 'blown', so the young dead at the battle of Mametz Wood seem to have been slaughtered without a chance of survival. Facing a barrage of fire from 'nesting machine guns' they had been 'told to walk not run' over unfamiliar territory to their deaths. **2** The foreign soil is personified. It has watched over the bodies 'for years' and now pushes them towards the surface, 'like a wound working a foreign body to the surface of the skin'. The Welsh soldiers don't belong in France and Sheers suggests that the soil exposes 'the broken mosaic of bone linked arm in arm' to remind people many years later of the futility of war. **3**

Wilfred Owen actually named his poem 'Futility' to make his feelings clear about the heartbreaking loss of life in the First World War. **4** He, unlike Sheers, writes his

---

1 Point, example, explanation

2 Detail linked to interpretation

3 Considers effectiveness of technique
4 Considered response to structure
5 Developed comparison of poets' uses of form and explanation of choice
This response thoughtfully links detail to the poet's use of figurative language and compares the choice of form with some detail. For a higher grade it needs to analyse the uses of techniques more closely, in developed detail, concentrating on interpreting their effects on the reader and exploring possible alternative meanings

1 Explores idea

2 Close analysis of technique to support interpretation and effect on reader

3 Evaluates poet's use of technique
4 Succinct comparison of poets' purposes

---

poem in two stanzas, the first beginning with the command to move the body of the dead comrade 'into the sun'. The warmth from 'the kind old sun' will surely wake up the sleeping soldier, in the way it always has, by 'whispering of fields unsown' when there was farm work to be done. Any hope, however, is soon lost in the second stanza when cold reality kicks in. **5** The speaker, in the persona perhaps of the dead man's friend, cries out despairingly 'Are limbs, so dear-achieved, too hard to stir?' The words 'still warm' are surrounded by dashes to emphasise the realisation that the young man was alive so recently, yet is now far away from any chance of a future life. **6** 'Mametz Wood' doesn't share the bitterness or despair of 'Futility' and the sad reflective mood of the poem doesn't seem to change. Sheers gives a moving description of the soldiers' skeletons linked 'arm in arm' in one long single stanza. The account begins in storytelling style with 'For years afterwards' and ends with the haunting picture of 'socketed heads' with jaws 'dropped open'. The discovery of the skeletons now allows the horror of their deaths to speak out. Their 'absent tongues' can, at last, question why they were sacrificed. **7**

5 Evaluates effect of form

6 Imaginative interpretation of effectiveness of punctuation

7 Evaluative comparison of form and effects on reader

Relationships

Writing about poets' purposes and ideas

3 Compare how feelings towards another person are shown in 'To his coy mistress' and one other poem in 'Relationships'.

C-grade response

In 'To his coy mistress' a young man tries to persuade his girlfriend to sleep with him. **1** He pretends that he would wait hundreds and thousands of years for her if there was 'world enough, and time'. He works his way through each part of her body, telling her she deserves to be praised for each part, before the frightening second stanza, where he describes her dead in a 'marble vault'. 'But none, I think, do there embrace' **2** he says, trying to convince her that there is no time to waste. **3**

When he writes 'and your quaint honour turn to dust' I think he is making fun of her because she wants to stay a virgin. **4** He says 'and into ashes all my lust' and that's why he's trying to frighten her — he's full of lust and doesn't really love her. **5** At the end of the poem he writes 'Now let us sport us while we may' so it's clear why he is trying to frighten her with scary details of what happens to you when you die. The only reason for all his persuasion is to get his girlfriend into bed. **6**

In 'The farmer's bride' Charlotte Mew also writes about a man who would like a woman to share his bed, but in this poem it's his wife. **7** The farmer spends so much time on the farm with his animals, he doesn't know how to treat a woman. His new wife, who is very young, is terrified of him. He says: 'When us was wed she turned

1 Makes the point of poet's purpose

2 Supporting quotations

3 Undeveloped explanation

4 Links detail to interpretation

5 Personal interpretation

6 Interpretation linked to poet's purpose

7 Comparison of poets' themes

8 Develops idea

9 Point lacks example and further explanation

10 Thoughtful consideration of idea, but lacks development

11 Compares similarity in theme

afraid/of love and me and all things human'. **8** The young girl runs away but she's brought back and locked up to stop her from running away again. **9** I don't think the farmer loves her. He likes the way she looks with her brown eyes and her hair and at the end of the poem all he can think about is how she is sleeping above him. He says "tis but a stair betwixt us". **10** The women in both poems refuse to sleep with the men. In 'Coy mistress', she is probably afraid of losing her reputation, but in 'Farmer's bride' she's too scared of the rough farmer, who she doesn't know properly. **11**

A*-grade response

Marvell in 'To his coy mistress' skilfully presents a three-part argument as to why a young woman should sleep with his young male persona. He begins by assuring her that if there was 'but world enough, and time' then both would be thoroughly used for praise and adoration of physical beauty. 'You deserve this state' he grovels, to try and get her on his side and then he pounces with his terrifying description of bodily disintegration when 'worms shall try/That long preserved virginity'. **1** 'Time's winged chariot' won't wait, he explains, before playing his ace in the final stanza. 'Now...while your willing soul transpires...let us sport us' he exclaims, and the reader can imagine his overconfident conviction that his mistress is impressed. She hasn't said she's 'willing' — yet, but he's assured his argument cannot fail. **2**

1 Explores interpretation of detail

2 Perceptive evaluation of effects of language

The poem, written in the seventeenth century, is still greatly enjoyed in the twenty-first century. It has geographical and religious detail which set it in its own time, with the exotic idea of rubies from the East and a reference to Christian and Jewish differences, yet its purpose, that is, at which point a relationship should become physical, is contemporary. **3** Marvell's mistress' 'quaint virginity' would have been considered necessary for her to find a good husband, and the voice of the persona would surely have been aware of this. Therefore the poem was probably written as a metaphysical game to prove a clever argument, rather than a desperate attempt to 'tear our pleasures with rough strife'. **4**

3 Explores poetic purpose and ideas

4 Convincing and imaginative interpretation

There is a hint in 'The farmer's bride' that the young bride was not 'coy' but terrified of sex with her new husband. The farmer describes her as 'Lying awake with her wide brown stare'. It isn't surprising to the reader that the 'maid, too young maybe' was so frightened of her strange uncommunicative husband that she 'runned away'. **5** The farmer's lack of guilt when he describes how 'We caught her, fetched her home at last/And turned the key upon her, fast', turns the modern reader against this cruel man, who can only recognise beauty and grace in nature, but can't be sensitive and romantic with his young wife who is 'shy as a leveret'. **6** Marvell's young speaker, on the other hand, is full of romantic persuasive skills, which is why his suggestion: 'Let us roll all our strength and all/Our sweetness

5 Evaluates personal interpretation

6 Evaluates reader response to theme, with detail

up into one ball' is far more likely to succeed with a reluctant lady. The 'frightened fay' as the seasons progress, will not warm to her desperate husband. To get her smile back he would have to learn to talk to her. **7**

7 Consistent convincing comparison

Writing about poetic techniques and their effect on the reader

> 4 Compare how poets express their feelings for another member of their family in 'Nettles' and one other poem from 'Relationships'.'.

C-grade response

Vernon Scannell describes the nettles which hurt his son as though they are an enemy army. He calls them 'that regiment of spite behind the shed'. **1** This metaphor continues through the poem, when he calls them 'that fierce parade' and 'the fallen dead'. It's as though he is fighting an enemy and has to win the battle. At the end of the poem he describes the new nettles which have grown as 'tall recruits'. The reader knows how the father must feel as nettle stings really hurt and the three year old would not understand. **2** But both parents are able to comfort the little boy, because he is so young. When he is older they know they won't be able to comfort him as much, because the 'sharp wounds' you get when you're grown up are harder to deal with than nettle stings. **3**

1 Point and example

2 Developed explanation of effect of metaphor on the reader

3 Details linked to interpretation

In the same way that the language in 'Nettles' has a military theme, and uses military metaphors, 'Harmonium' has a theme of ageing. **4** The church organ is no longer needed and Armitage and his father turn up to carry it away. It is very sad that the organ which has produced such lovely music over a hundred years should now be old. Its case is 'aged' and its keys are 'yellowed' like an elderly person. **5** The poet's father is also getting old, 'with smoker's fingers and dottled thumbs' and he knows that one day soon he will have to be carried out of the church in a coffin. His son just mumbles to his father 'some shallow or sorry phrase' because he doesn't know what to say when his father talks about dying. **6** Both 'Harmonium' and 'Nettles' have an extra surprise thought at the end, but the difference is that in one the son is thinking about his father in the future and in the other the father is thinking about his son's future. **7**

4 Comparison of themed language

5 Appreciates use of personification

6 Develops idea of ageing

7 Comparison of endings, but lacks detail

A*-grade response

Scannell uses an extended military metaphor throughout 'Nettles' to put across his parental anger at his young son's distress, when the three year old falls into a 'bed' of nettles and the 'green spears' become 'a regiment of spite behind the shed'. Scannell commences his own crusade, deciding he must conquer 'that fierce parade' and 'the fallen dead' are given their own 'funeral pyre'. **1** Perhaps the

1 Explores technique concisely with detail

father's actions seem over-dramatic, yet the 'white blisters beaded on his tender skin' make the young child sound innocent and vulnerable. Surely any parent would empathise with the father who can only comfort his son and give a visual display of retribution by slashing 'in fury' at a patch of weeds. **2**

2 Convincing interpretation of effectiveness of language

'Harmonium' also seems to be an autobiographical account of a father and son incident, yet the poet's reflections in this second poem are those of the son towards the ageing father, not the father considering his growing son. Similarly to the battle-theme of 'Nettles' a theme of ageing runs through Armitage's poem, crossing over from descriptions of the redundant Chapelette to the father with 'smoker's fingers and dottled thumbs', who morbidly comments on his own approaching death. **3** The personified organ, that has 'lost its tongue' with its 'yellowed fingernails', contrasts movingly with a time when the harmonium accompanied the melodious voices of generations of fathers and sons, so that 'gilded finches…had streamed out'. This delightful image of golden songbirds flying through the church precedes the more sombre last verse, reminding the reader that time brings changes, as the organ is carried out 'flat, laid on its back'. **4** The poem ends with a feeling of regret that the son isn't able to provide a comforting response to his father's droll, yet probably apprehensive, observation that he'd be the next 'dead weight' to be carried through the church. **5** 'Nettles' also ends with a tone of regret. The father, who can so easily comfort a child, after a brief unpleasantness, recognises that the 'sharp wounds' of adult pain, usually caused by troubled relationships, are not so easily 'soothed' by a loving parent. **6**

3 Evaluates and compares uses of language

4 Close analysis of detail

5 Insightful personal response

6 Evaluative comparison

PHILIP ALLAN LITERATURE GUIDE **FOR GCSE**